When a red kitten claws its way up her gown while she's out gathering wood, Emer Drumwiddy knows her true love will come to her in eight years' time. It seems a long time to wait, as she's already twenty-two. Living alone since her mother married a leprechaun man from far-off Erin a' Fee, Emer is happy to adopt Red for company. She just doesn't bargain on getting Rory as well.

Rory is an orphan, and he loves Emer from the first time he sees her. As he grows to manhood, he begins to love her in a different way.

Emer is fond of her wee laddie, but the eight years are nearly up. What will Rory do when her true love comes to claim her?

Emer
Copyright © 2020 Lark Westerly
ISBN: 978-1-4874-2945-4
Cover art by Martine Jardin

Published by eXtasy Books Inc or
Devine Destinies, an imprint of eXtasy Books Inc

Look for us online at:
www.eXtasybooks.com or www.devinedestinies.com

EMER
THE RED CAT BOOK 1

BY

LARK WESTERLY

Author Notes

The *Fairy in the Bed* series spans several decades and a great many characters who wander in and out of one another's stories. One frequently appearing character is the reverend Rory Inkersoll, grandfather of Duffy Inkersoll of *Pen and Ink*.

The *Red Cat* series tells Rory's story, first through the eyes of his beloved Emer, and later through his own, and through the clear gaze of Beatrice Hammett, a redoubtable pisky minx.

This series runs in parallel with the *Pixie Grip* series, which follows the lives of the Peckerdale Grene clan.

For those who wonder where reality meets invention, *Roses of Picardy* is a real song, but the film *Violet in Paradise* is made up. Catsear is a real plant. Its botanical name is *Hypochaeris radicata*. Stepaway Falls, Shipley, Patterdale and Appledore are all invented places, but the big flood John Folly mentions did occur. The conversation Emer overhears when she first sees the ring box via *the sight* comes from a scene in *Love Began at Christmas*.

CHAPTER ONE: THE RED KITTEN

December 1944, *The Pixie Forest, Over There*

Emer Drumwiddy looked down at the small creature clinging to her skirts. She wore good braeside wool, so the rose-prickle claws would do no harm to her clothing. She was less confident about her skin.

The kitten yowled and stared up at her with wide, amber eyes.

"I wondered when you'd show up, wee mannie." Her voice sounded oddly calm to her, but then . . . how could she feel excited about something eight years in her future?

She bent and unhooked the kitten's claws from her skirt before she lifted it to eye-level.

Its eyes widened, and its pink mouth opened in silent appeal.

"Och, you poor wee mannie."

Emer brought the ginger scrap to her breast and rested it against her bosom. "What am I to do with you, now you've come?"

The kitten snuggled in and implied it had some ideas, possibly involving a warm place to sleep and a lap for comfortable kneading.

Emer adjusted her shawl, conjuring it into a sling. The kitten purred, rubbing its whiskered cheek against the swell of her breast.

Emer blinked, startled by the caress, if that was what it was. She'd known the red kitten would come to her someday, but until then it had been a concept, not a solid little mass of fur and purr.

She bent to gather an armful of broken branches from the undergrowth where she'd dropped it when the kitten leapt from wherever it had been hiding to swing from her skirt.

Didn't see that detail.

She chuckled and walked on over the brae and down into the glen and then to the pixie forest and along to the edge of the green way.

Emer didn't know why she'd built her cottage so far from the braelands. It had just seemed the best place to be. She didn't know why she'd left the house where she'd been born, and where she'd lived for most of her life. She went there now and again, and she walked through the sleeping rooms to be sure all was well.

Her mother's furniture was still there, and so were some of her gowns of braeside wool. Sometimes when Emer went to visit she'd note a gown missing, or a treasured piece of crockery no longer on the dresser. In the early days, there had often been notes waiting there for her to find.

Darling Emer . . . they'd begin, and they'd end *with all our love until the Lord sees fit for us to meet again.*

Emer never wrote back. How could she? It was enough to know Dornie was well and happy.

She opened the swinging gate and let herself into her garden. It was a young planting. The pinecone she'd set by the gate had lately put up a hopeful spike of green. The flower beds had ankle-deep plants. She wanted them higher, knee deep and thigh deep. She was greedy for the bees to hum in waist-high lavender.

"Everything to its time," she said aloud. She had got into the habit of talking to herself, in the time she'd been living alone.

She entered the cottage and sniffed the scent of new timber. Her friend, Catriona Mcdonald Chaucer, had helped her with some of the work, and so had Cat's cheery band of brothers and cousins, all fine braefolk men with heathered eyes and rough thatches of hair ranging from black to almost blond. When the work was done, the men had all crowded into the kitchen and stood in a circle, backs to the walls, arms folded over broad chests, all smiling at her.

"Aye?" She'd looked them over with a lifted brow.

Cat, hand-in-hand with her new husband, Humphrey Chaucer, said mischievously, "They're waiting for you to pick one o' them, hen."

"For what?"

"To wed! Right, laddies?"

The men all nodded solemnly. Emer thought they were amused, but also willing to play along.

"I've a kiss o' friendship for you all, but no more than that," she said.

They sighed in unison.

"I never promised anything else."

The man to her right, whose name was Douglas Mcdonald, held out his arms. She went to kiss him. He gave her a hug. "Bless you, lassie, I'd have liked it fine if you could ha' chosen me," he said in her ear, and he handed her on to his brother, Callum.

Round the kitchen she went, kissing, hugging and thanking Mcdonalds, Gordons, MacHeathers and an Irving. They were all fine laddies, braw, fit, kind and loving. They smelled of furze and heather, rain and barley.

"Any lassie who takes one of you for her man will be blessed among women," she said to them all.

"So why not you, Emer?" Cat sounded disappointed. Emer knew Cat had hoped they might become sisters or cousins-by-love at the least.

She smiled. "I can take no man to my bed. The red kitten's no' come yet."

3

She fed them scones, and they played their pipes to warm the cottage. Then they all bade her farewell and ranged off home.

Emer sighed. One day she'd find the love of her life. *The sight* told her that. It didn't show her his face or form. Instead, it persisted in showing her a red kitten.

He'll come to ye first . . . the lover will be eight summers on.

Emer was twenty-one. It seemed a long time to wait, especially when she'd just closed the door on a dozen handsome men.

The sight had come through the Drumwiddy line. Her father's grandmother, who had wed her cousin, was said to have held it strongly. It had touched Emer in childhood, and her young mother, although not having it herself, had always treated it with respect.

And sometimes, Emer thought, in the quiet after her housewarming, it could be an unmitigated nuisance.

But here she was in her cottage, a few months later, and the red kitten, the precursor, had come. She was twenty-two today. If *the sight* was right, then she'd be thirty when *he* came to her.

At least I'll know him when he deigns to show his face at my door. I wonder, will he be as bonnie as the laddies Cat had for my inspection? Who knew the brae had such a crop of fine unpromised laddies?

She put wood into the stove, set the kettle on to boil, and conjured some oatcakes from the larder. She sat in her favourite chair, which was the rocker from the brae house, covered with her father's old plaid. David Drumwiddy had gone to glory when she was seventeen, but he'd been quite old when she was born. Her mother, his second wife, and very much younger than David, was wed to a leprechaun man now. She lived with him at far-off Erin a' Fee.

The manner of this wedding had taken even Emer by

surprise. *The sight* suggested some shift in the winds of her life, but it was maddeningly noncommittal. That generally meant she had a choice to make. She was always cautious about choices predicted by *the sight*. Almost always, they promised to impact heavily on someone she loved.

CHAPTER TWO: THE KELPIE

September 1943, *Dornie's cottage on the brae, Over There*

Emer and Dornie had put aside the quilt they'd been making. They'd drunk their tea and were winding wool on the porch when a green gossoon rode into the brae on a fair grey mare. The horse was one of the kelpie breed, which was startling enough. It was more startling when the man, in reply to their greeting, announced that he'd come to the brae to fetch the love of his life.

He dismounted from the mare and hitched her to the fence and then came to climb the steps to the porch. He was small, in the leprechaun fashion, but straight-backed and handsome. His fine hazel eyes ranged over Emer and then settled on Dornie, Emer's mother, who was sitting in her dead husband's rocker with a ball of wool in her hands. "Greet ye, my beauty! Will ye come wid me to the green way and be me own dear darlin'?"

Dornie glanced at Emer, who saw the agony of temptation in her mother's eyes.

This is the decision.

"Och, go with him if you've a mind to, Mam . . . Da gave you leave to be happy after he'd gone."

"It's been only a year since he went to glory . . . and I do not know this man. Och, it's impossible!"

"Your heart knows him, I do believe. His certainly knows yours."

Dornie looked into the hazel eyes. So did Emer, and saw

hope and kindness there and a kind of desperate daring, as if he'd screwed up his courage to ask for his heart's desire.

They belong together, the sight whispered. *He knows it. You know it, and your mam will know it if she gives herself leave.*

"If you go with him now, you can give me that wee sister I always wanted. Leave it much longer and there'll be no chance of her," Emer said firmly.

She kissed her mother and then the leprechaun man for good measure. "Now, laddie, I'll go to my friend Cat's and leave the two of you to get acquainted."

He huffed and informed her he was no laddie, but forty years old.

Braeside men were *laddies* from birth unto death. Emer remembered, a little too late, that leprechaun men were gossoons. To *them,* a laddie was a child.

"To be sure!" she said in the sweet leppy lilt. She'd always been a good mimic.

They laughed about it then.

He gave her a gift from the pack he carried. She was hesitant, but he said it was due to her as his daughter-by-love.

"What is that?" Emer asked, with interest, turning over the package to examine the green cloth wrapping.

"Sure, 'tis a kelpie bottle, darlin' Emer."

"I see," she said, laughing, although she wondered why one would want to bottle a kelpie. Anyway, how *could* one bottle a kelpie? She glanced at the grey mare and hoped it hadn't heard.

Dornie invited her suitor to take tea on the porch.

Emer, amused, nonplussed and with the pain of change upon her, ventured to unhitch the mare, which turned its back and sauntered over to eat the climbing beans.

Emer didn't dare to stop her.

Not wanting to disturb what must be the oddest courtship the brae had ever seen, she conjured her plaid and went to visit Catriona, who was still in the early days of her love affair with Humphrey.

Emer said nothing of her reason for the visit, and Cat asked no questions. She was caught up in her romance, and that was her main concern.

After supper, Humphrey came calling, so Emer walked on down to where the heather met the pixie forest and lay down under the stars.

"What in the world?" she asked the night.

The night had no answer, but *the sight* came to her, gently, bringing a picture of her mother transformed by joy, holding a rosy baby in her arms. The leprechaun man, whose name she still didn't know, looked on with tears in his eyes.

Joy cometh in the morning.

Emer remembered Master Grene, the pastor, saying that when he laid David Drumwiddy to rest. It was a quiet service, for apart from his widow and daughter, David was the last of his family. His first marriage, to a lady older than him, had been childless.

In the morning, not too early, Emer went home to make herself breakfast.

To her surprise, she found Dornie and the leprechaun man still sitting on the porch. They were holding hands, and Dornie had a tiny silver horseshoe pinned to her gown. The gossoon wore a bracelet of braided wool around his arm . . . some of the ball Dornie had been winding when he arrived.

They're promised.

"You'll be off then, Mam?" Emer said.

"Aye. It's decided . . . unless . . ."

"I want that wee sister," Emer reminded.

The leprechaun man gave her a brilliant smile. He whistled through his teeth, and the kelpie mare lifted her head from where she was demolishing the green peas. She came to the porch and snorted.

Dornie hugged Emer, with tears sliding down her cheeks. "Emer —"

"Hush, Mam. Everything is falling right."

The man lifted Dornie in strong arms and set her onto the mare.

"If iver ye truly need us, or anything else, darlin' Emer, write a wish on a paper, put it in the kelpie bottle I gave ye, and fling it into the waves," he said.

She conjured the gift from where she'd sent it into the kist for safekeeping before leaving to visit Cat. She took off the wrapping, and she looked it over. It was made of opalescent glass, and it was a curious shape her hands could tell though her eyes couldn't.

"What exactly is a kelpie bottle? I should have asked before, but I was a wee bit startled when you gave it to me first," she asked the gossoon.

"Indade, and how should ye not be? Rest easy, *iníon le grá.* A kelpie bottle is a powerful charm, and few folk ever see one. I had this from a lady o' Heather Isle, a friend of my mam, who swore she'd lost patience with me. Mam said I was to use it to choose a colleen and make a family."

"And you did?"

"I did not! I wrote me wish to find the love of me life, which is a different matter entirely."

"I suppose it is," Emer agreed.

"An' it brought me a kelpie who carried me here . . .'tis said the kelpies swim the wish to heaven and back and when the time is ripe, back it will come to your hand to keep and at that moment, your wish will turn from a hope to a truth."

"And you're giving this gift to me."

"I am. It can be used for any manner of wishes, but only once. Remember, ye're to use it for whativer ye need most. It is a great charm of power."

Emer promised and watched them ride away. Then she conjured the kelpie bottle back to the kist. She was still reeling from the speed with which her life had changed.

She had just one certainty in her sea of confusion. What had happened was *right* for the leprechaun man, for Dornie . . . and somehow, it was right for her.

Emer lived on in her old house for a year and then moved to the pixie forest where *the sight* said she needed to be for the next stage of her life.

Chapter Three: Summer Storm

December 1944, *The Pixie Forest, Over There*

The rocker creaked in a companionable song as Emer swayed in rhythm to her memories. She saw them play over in her mind, clear as pictures on the page. When she'd followed them to her wood-gathering and to its conclusion, she rose to make the tea.

Her shawl, weighted with the red kitten, swayed, warm against her breast.

Seated again, this time with tea in her favourite cup and the stove gently warming the room, Emer removed the shawl to her lap and unwrapped her new friend.

Looking him over, she saw he was about half grown. That was good, since he'd be able to deal with his personal grooming and not need a titty bottle to feed. He was asleep, with his claws hooked into the shawl, as she discovered when she tried to lift him from her lap.

"No need to hang on, wee mannie. I'll not put you out unless you want to go."

The kitten released his grip and mewed himself awake.

"I daresay I have something to feed you. Master Peckerdale brought me fish from Mistress Jestima when I sent her the salve."

She felt the small stomach and judged the kitten had eaten recently. Yet she had no sense that he belonged to anyone in particular. He felt as if he'd been suddenly cut adrift.

I was cut adrift a year ago . . .

"Maybe you're a barn cat's son, and off to seek your own way?" she suggested. To be sure, he seemed a little young for that.

She drank her tea, and he purred in her lap until supper time. They shared the fish, stewed up with carrots and tatties from her mother's old garden, and Emer walked around her new one, encouraging her plantings to grow strong and green.

The evening drew into night, and she went back into the cottage and prepared to sleep.

She put the kitten on the pillow beside her, in case he needed company in the night, but he wouldn't stay.

"Sleep by the stove then," she said, amused. She conjured her old childhood plaid, now stuffed with springyweed, out of the kist and spread it a safe distance from the stove.

The kitten gazed at her, wide-eyed.

"Sleep there if ye please," she said, and she got into bed in her petticoat.

She was half asleep when she heard the kitten brush against her rocking chair.

I should let him out . . .

She was too tired to get up, reasoning that a small puddle would be easy enough to deal with.

When she woke in the morning, the red kitten had gone.

Emer was perplexed, as she'd closed the windows against the cool night air. He was such a wee creature she thought he might be hiding away somewhere, but a thorough search failed to find him.

"Well, I knew he'd come. I never thought he mightn't stay," she said aloud. It was a while since she'd had anyone to talk to. Catriona came to visit sometimes, but now that she was Mistress Chaucer, she had other things on her mind. Besides, she'd not quite forgiven Emer for rejecting the chance to join her family.

She hadn't said so, but it had been in her eyes. *It's not as if you have one of your own . . .*

Emer put on her gown and went about her business for the day.

At midday, she returned to the cottage with some beeswax to pound with herbs to make more salve. She found the kitten purring on her bed.

Emer put down her basket, surprised and amused at how pleased she was to see him. She lifted him into her lap, and they spent an hour in friendly contact before she began to compound her ingredients.

The kitten stayed until evening closed in, when it settled by the stove. As before, it was gone in the morning.

Emer shrugged and accepted him as her *sometimes cat.*

Things went on this way until one evening when a summer storm blew up.

Emer lay in bed listening to the stinging rain and wind.

"I wonder if ye'll be off into this, wee mannie?" she said aloud.

The kitten stalked restlessly about. After a while, she ceased to see his small shadow and knew he'd gone out, somehow.

He wasn't gone long. A sneeze and a cross snuffle announced he was back, and she saw him outlined against the glow of the stove, licking the wet from his fur.

The storm continued unabated and was still raging in the morning when Emer got up to put wood in the stove.

An unseasonable chill had crept into the cottage, and she wrapped her shawl around her as she bent to pick up the wood. The room was almost dark, so she shuffled her feet carefully, not wanting to step on the kitten. She located the plaid and stepped around the end of it only to trip over something in the dark.

"Glory be to the saints!" she exclaimed, catching at the chair to save herself from falling.

"Holy mother with you," a voice out of the dark

responded. "Are you harmed, mistress?"

Chapter Four: Rory

1944, *The Pixie Forest, Over There*

Emer gasped and clicked her fingers to light the lantern. She supposed she should have done that before instead of moving about in the dark.

She blinked in the sudden light and straightened away from the chair.

A boy sat watching her from the plaid. He had red hair, amber eyes and a lithe little body folded up in a huddle.

He was stark naked, and after a shocked moment, Emer tossed him her shawl.

His wide gaze swivelled away from her, and she quickly conjured another and draped herself decently.

He looked back at her, and they eyed one another in silence for a while. Then Emer roused herself.

"I never saw this coming, wee mannie," she remarked.

He dropped his gaze, shyly.

"I beg your pardon, mistress. Mum always said there's nothing wrong with being bare, but it's not right for company . . . unless you're treefolk or waterfolk, of course." He looked up again. "You're a braesider?"

"Good guess. How did you know?"

"You have a plaidie, and big . . . um . . ."

"Big hips and titties?"

"That."

Emer smiled at him and put the wood in the stove. "I'll make tea, wee —"

15

"Not so wee," he said.

"You're not, are you?"

She sat in her chair and looked him over. He'd sat up and pulled the shawl around him. "If you look away, I can dress myself."

"Do that, then." Emer solemnly lifted her shawl in front of her eyes and stayed like that until he said, "Thank you, mistress."

"Emer," she said, putting the shawl to rights.

"Mistress Emer."

He'd dressed himself in britches and a pixie tunic, and retained the shawl, which he held in his lap, absently rubbing the wool against his cheek. He looked older than she'd first thought, but he was definitely a child rather than a young man.

"Have you a name to give me in return for mine?" she asked.

"I'm Rory."

"A fine name. It means red-headed, and so you are."

He nodded seriously. "Mum gave me the name on that account. She said my hair alone made *a joyful noise unto the Lord.* She said it was as close as she could get to calling me *Rose.* That was what she meant to call a daughter if she'd had one."

"How old are you, Rory?"

"I'm nine—no, ten."

"That's older than I thought at first."

"Yes." He wrinkled his nose. "It's a funny age. I was nine, and then I was nearly ten and then—this happened."

"This?" She had a good idea of what he meant.

"The manifestation." He brought out the word with care. "Mum didn't know, or at least, she didn't tell me. She did say I might not get old very fast, and she said I might just possibly have a kind of—um—*maid* self, and that would be just fine. But she didn't think so."

"You have some sylvan ancestry?" That was a pretty safe guess. As far as she knew, sylvan were the only bi-morphic order.

"Um. A bit. Maybe. Mum wasn't sure." His pale cheeks went pink. "Mum was wonderful. She loved me. She said love is the most important thing, and she said I was made with love. She told me I should always remember that."

"Undoubtedly so. You could *not* have been made without love."

That was clearly the right thing to say in the long term. In the short term, his amber eyes glowed with tears, and his firm little mouth went crooked.

"I beg your pardon, mistress. I have to . . ." His voice faded as he drew himself in and became the red kitten.

Emer leaned forward and picked him up, stroking and gentling him. "Poor wee mannie. Poor wee—" She hesitated to name the kitten *Rory*. From the little she knew of mutable fay of this degree, the red kitten and the child were not entirely the same being. "Poor wee Red," she said. She sat holding the kitten until it went to sleep. She was about to put it to rest on the chair while she made her long-awaited tea when it stirred and stretched and abruptly fell off her lap.

"Oh!"

Biting her lip, Emer clicked out the light and dropped her second shawl over where she thought the child must have landed.

This is going to be inconvenient . . . for him.

Despite the storm, she heard him shifting and rustling about. She got up cautiously to get the tea.

"Put the light on if you want," he said.

She did so. "Would you like some tea? Or would you rather have milk?"

"Tea please with milk in it. I like milk and cheese."

She poured a second cup and topped it up with milk before handing it to him. Then, smiling to herself, she conjured oatcakes out of the crock, topped one with a slice of cheese, and handed him that as well.

"Thank you. I wasn't hinting, though."

"Och, it wouldn't matter if you were. Growing laddies need good food."

They drank in silence, and then Emer said, "Rory, I need to ask this. Please do not think I'm being too curious."

"Go ahead, mistress."

"I think you should call me Emer."

"Should I? Aren't you a grown lady?"

"I'm a braefolk lassie . . . mostly. My great-granny was a colleen, called Emer Brightstep. I am named for her. I think you probably have some leprechaun in you, too?"

"Yes. And brae, and a bit of teg. Some pixie. Mum had a kind of cousin whose name is Corrie. *She's* a colleen. I met her twice, and I liked her a lot. I don't know where she is now. I wish I did."

"There, then! What was her other name?"

He cast his gaze down in thought. "It was a name that Mum said had something to do with rings. I don't remember it."

Leprechauns chose their own last names when they were in their teens, and the resulting appellations ranged from a simple statement of aptitude or appearance to complicated polysyllables that no one but another leprechaun could translate.

She said, "You might see her again one day. And maybe you and I are related."

"Not very, I expect."

"Is anyone going to worry that you didn't come home last night?"

He shook his head too quickly.

"Rory?"

"My guardian said I should learn to be both parts of me.

He said if I needed to be out, I could go. He said cats were *unconfinable.* I think that was a joke."

"He probably did not mean you should stay out all night, though."

He screwed up his face. "It was stormy."

"It still is. Can you conjure yet?"

"I conjured my clothes!"

"So you did. You must be an early learner. Here's what we're going to do. I will write a message to your guardian and let him know you're staying safely with me until the storm clears. Will you give me his name?"

"He's a pixie man named Master Berryman Grene. His lady is named Mistress Clover. They're very kind. Mum said they were good folk and godly."

"I know Master Grene. He's a pastor," she said.

"Yes! That's why Mum asked him to be my guardian before she went to glory."

His eyes glazed again, and Emer said quickly, "I think she made a good choice, laddie. I'll write to Master Grene and tell him you're safe here and that you're welcome to come to me whenever you want a change of company."

She conjured paper and ink and wrote the message, which she folded and signed, trusting the Grenes would remember her. She and Dornie hadn't attended many services, but Berryman Grene had been as kind as could be when they asked him to say the words for David.

She handed the letter to Rory. "Conjure this to where Master Grene will see it easily. Then we'll have breakfast. When the storm eases, you can go home."

Rory held the paper and closed his eyes. For a few moments, nothing happened, and then it vanished.

"Done!"

"Very good." She smiled at him to soften her next words. "Rory, if you're going to keep on visiting me, we need some rules. First, I have to know how you come and go without opening the door or window."

He worried his lip, frowning. "I don't know. Master Grene says my manifestation might be a stealth cat. He can go through walls. *I* can't."

"I see. Well, the red kitten is welcome to come and go through my walls, but *you*, Master Rory, will tap on the door. You will also not enter my tub room while I am in there."

"I won't."

"On the other hand, I don't want you to be worried if you happen to be bare when you wake up after a nap. Your mam was right. Bodies are wonderful things. I know you're not a water lad or treefolk, but you *are* highly mutable, and that puts you into a different order from most folk. So, if it happens, you can just conjure your clothing. I won't be worried or embarrassed, and you shouldn't be either."

"But what if you—"

"I'm usually dressed, but as I said, you stay out of the tub room unless I give you leave to have a tub yourself, or . . . in case you need privacy to change to *this* self."

He said he would.

"One last thing. If you ever need to see me, or if you just need a hug, come along. The red kitten is always welcome to sit with me if I'm not busy with something else. If you find you don't want to see me again, then that's fine, too. I won't be hurt or offended—not a scrap. Come or not, whatever makes you and your red kitten happy." She gave him another smile. "Those are my rules. Do you have some for me?"

"Just one. Please don't call me *wee*."

She put out her hand, and he laid his in it. "It's a bargain."

CHAPTER FIVE: GOOD COMPANIONS

1947, *The Pixie Forest, Over There*

Emer grew used to having Rory around. He usually came to visit in his red kitten form, but he'd morph into his lad form when Emer made the tea.

He was good company in both morphs, affectionate but independent. After three years of their acquaintanceship, she found she enjoyed his visits for their conversations and for practical help, too. At thirteen he was as tall as she was, and his cat-self, though still lean and gangling, was close to full-grown.

The first time he rubbed his cheek against her knee while sitting by the stove, she was startled, but she remembered in time that the red cat was a part of him. He'd been sketching with a piece of charcoal, but had put aside the work, relaxed his shoulders, and stretched, bringing his cheek closer to her chair to rub against her. When he did it again, she said gently, "Rory," and waited until he looked up into her face.

"Yes?"

"What you just did then . . ."

He looked confused and glanced at his drawing.

"No' that." She reached down and rubbed her fingers across his cheek.

"Oh." He leaned away. "I'm sorry."

"No need to be sorry, laddie. I just wondered why."

"Why what?"

She sighed. "Do you ever play with other—I mean with

cats that are always cats?"

"Mistress Clover has a kitchen tabby called Vashti. I roll a ball for her sometimes."

"That's not quite what I meant. I mean, when you're in cat form, do you play with cats? Hunt with them? Wrestle in the straw, maybe?"

He blushed.

"It's quite all right if you do."

"I don't. They won't. They don't like me. They go all—" He stiffened, developed a fixed stare and stretched his fingers into claws. He hissed.

Emer drew back a little, trying to hide her shock.

Rory relaxed and gave her a reproachful look. "They know the red cat's not properly a cat. And now you know I'm not properly a lad."

"Of *course* you are." She held out her arms, but he shuffled away and soon went home.

He left his sketch lying by the stove, and Emer picked it up. It was a picture of a dog—a spaniel, she thought—standing with paw upraised, gazing at a figure in the distance. It was beautifully rendered in just a few strokes and some shading. Emer admired it, and then she put it carefully away in the old kist, in case Rory asked for it later. She wondered where he'd met the dog.

He didn't come back for a week, and Emer was tempted to visit his guardian to find out if he was all right.

Master Grene and his lady had called on her casually soon after the storm. Mistress Grene was in need of some of Emer's marigold salve, having heard of it from Mistress Peckerdale. They stayed for tea and soda bread and discussed Emer's burgeoning garden. They asked after Dornie, and Mistress Grene admired a quilted cushion Emer had made for her rocking chair. Nothing was said about Rory's visits, but these continued, so Emer assumed they found her a fit companion for their ward.

The only reason she didn't return their visit when he stayed away was because of the bargain she'd made with Rory. He was welcome to visit her, or not. Having her visit him wasn't part of the arrangement.

When he finally came back, he arrived in his lad form and tapped on the door.

Emer let him in.

He said, "If I do anything inappropriate, or if I act like a cat when I'm *me*, please tell me."

"Och, but you never do anything inappropriate. You're one of the nicest laddies I know."

"Thanks, but I know I can be odd. I have lessons at the castle with some other lads and maids, and they think I'm strange. Gia Oak said my eyes are funny."

"That was a wee bit personal," Emer said.

"Oh, Gia wasn't being unkind. Her mother's a courtfolk lady, but her dad's a tree lad. You know how those folk say whatever's in their heads. It's never mean. She said she liked my funny eyes and she asked me if I used them to see pretty things."

Emer wondered how under the heavens a courtfolk lady had come to have a child with a treefolk man. And then, of course, she chided herself for lack of charity. Treefolk were like waterfolk, kindly and sweet-natured. Why would a court lady *not* have been happy to love one for a while, or even forever?

"You have beautiful eyes, but I would never call them *funny*."

"She meant the way I—um—" He blinked and looked straight at her.

She looked back, neither up or down, because they were the same height. His pupils widened and then settled into narrow bands of darkness in the amber iris.

"I see."

He looked away. "Cats do that. It makes people feel odd to see a lad do it."

"I suppose it might trouble a few folk to see that, but it's not anything you need to worry about."

"Tell me when I do it . . . or the other thing." She didn't ask what that was, but he tilted his face and rubbed his cheek against hers. "That."

"I will then. It didn't trouble me, if that's what you were thinking, but . . . why *do* you do that to folk?"

"I don't . . . I mean, I don't think I've ever done it before that time. At least, I don't remember. I didn't do it . . ." He paused, frowning, and then said, "consciously."

"Then there's no need to worry."

He shrugged and moved away. "I brought you something." He laid a small shiny object on the scrubbed table and stood back.

Emer came over to look and picked up a piece of quartz in a subtle pink. "Thank you. It's beautiful. Where did you find it?"

"A pisky man I know had some to swap. He makes rings and pins for folk, but he had lots of crystals an alpman trades with him, and he gave me this."

"May I ask what you swapped?"

He gave her a shy grin and looked away. "He's called Master Jago Pendennis. He's a mutie like me, but his manifestation is a dog."

"I don't know him."

"He's over in the pisky hills. Master Grene said I should talk to him because he could help me with the cat thing. So, I'm going to see him each week."

"Rory, what did you swap?"

"Well, I didn't climb a tree so he could chase me!" He flashed her another grin. "I made him oatcakes, the way you showed me."

"I'm sure he enjoyed them. You're a fine baker." She held the quartz to the light. "It has a hole through it."

"That's so you can hang it from the window, or around your neck. Mum used to wear a teeny wooden rose on a ribbon around her neck."

She went on staring at the crystal, but she wasn't seeing it anymore. She was seeing a grey mare galloping over a hill carrying a tall lassie with the Drumwiddy plaid wrapped around her shoulders.

"Emer?" She blinked, aware that Rory was staring at her.

She shook herself. "I just had a touch of the *sight*."

"Did you see another kitten coming to trouble your life?"

"No, I saw a kelpie mare and me riding her. I think I'll be going away for a while to see my mam. I told you she went away to marry a leprechaun man. It's a long while since I saw her."

He looked stricken, and she recalled it was a long time since he'd seen his own mother, and that he had no hope of seeing her again.

It could not be unsaid, so she looked away from his face and back into the crystal.

"How long will you be away?" His voice was steady.

"I don't know. Could be a good while. You see, I have a wee sister to meet. I was waiting until she was old enough to know me, but it seems I'm being sent for."

"I'll miss you."

"I'll miss you, too, laddie." She conjured some wool from her kist and threaded it through the crystal. "I'll wear this and . . . see?" She held it up, smiling, and cast a glamour into the crystal.

Rory came to see. "That's a red cat."

"That's *your* red cat. I can show my wee sister my not-so-wee friend."

He took the crystal and hung it around her neck. "I'll be with you in spirit. I'll ask the Lord to bless you and your wee sister."

She said, "I hope you'll come to the cottage sometimes while I'm away. Light the fire to keep away the damp. Take anything from the garden that you want. You can read, or draw . . . brew tea, or bake . . ."

He nodded. "I'll come."

She thought he'd come a few times and then forget. He was old enough to be sponsored *over there* for a while, to learn human ways. She had no idea if the Grenes had made such arrangements for him, but they should find it easy enough. Master Grene was the pastor at the gateway church, so he must know a good many humans and halflings *over there* who would be happy to mentor a delightful laddie who was also a red cat.

CHAPTER SIX: FASH

1947, *The Pixie Forest, Over There*

The kelpie mare arrived at the cottage two weeks later. Emer eyed her with trepidation. She knew how to ride, but kelpies were unnerving creatures and exceedingly rare. They looked like horses, but their manner was *other*. It didn't help that the creature had no saddle or bridle.

She wondered if it was the same one who had carried her mother and the leprechaun man away some years before. It looked the same, but then she'd never seen more than the one.

"If I get on your back, my lass, will you carry me kindly or will you dump me in the furze?" she asked.

The mare tossed her head.

"Don't you try to intimidate me. I have a crystal from a friend to keep me safe."

She looked doubtfully at the creature.

"How am I to get on your back?"

"I should think she'll have to kneel," Rory said from behind her.

She turned to smile, while the mare gave a disagreeable snort. She was glad Rory had come in time to say farewell. "But will she kneel to a braeside lassie?"

"Maybe, if I have a word."

Before she could answer, he folded down into the red cat, rubbed once around her ankles and padded up to the mare. He chirruped. The mare lowered her head and sniffed at him.

He chirruped again, and she whickered and nudged him

gently.

He arched his back and bounced up to rub against her fore-leg.

Emer watched curiously as the wordless communication went on. She could only imagine what was happening between them on the *other* level. When Rory reassumed his lad form, he was smiling.

"Her name is a long one I can't pronounce, but she will answer to *Fash.*"

"Will she indeed!"

He shrugged. "She doesn't care for lads with red hair, or for men with black hair. You are a brown-haired lassie, so she will carry you safely in exchange for oatcakes every day."

"How does she know I have oatcakes?"

"Red told her. Your mum makes them, too, and Fash says yours had better be as good as those."

The mare snaked her head at him, and he backed away.

"That is, she didn't *say* it, precisely. It's difficult to explain."

"I hope my supply holds out for the journey."

"It will. I'll make sure of it."

"Thank you for that." Emer held out her hand, and he took it. Then he fished in his pocket and gave her another crystal. "For your little sister. Tell her the red cat wishes her well and hopes to meet her one day."

"So I will. What did you swap for this one?"

"A drawing for Master Pendennis's wife."

He didn't elaborate, so Emer tucked the crystal into her shawl and approached the mare. "Greet you, Fash."

The kelpie flicked her ears.

"If I try to get on your back without a stirrup, it will be an ungraceful scramble."

Snort. The mare bent her knees. Emer got onto her back and settled as well as she could. She glanced at Rory. "Did this beast tell you how I am to steer?"

"I don't think you do. You just sit there. She'll take you safely to where you're going."

"It's a village known as Rósanna Locha, in a place called Erin a' Fee."

"She'll take you there because she wants to go home. She has a friend waiting. And I *will* make sure the oatcake stocks are kept up. I promise."

"Thank you." Her smile slipped as Fash leapt to her full height and pranced.

Rory put his hand to her muzzle and dodged a snap. "Mistress Fash, please care for my queen."

"Your — ow!" Emer's question ended in a gasp as the kelpie bounded forward.

CHAPTER SEVEN: ERIN A' FEE

1948-50, *Rósanna Locha, Erin a' Fee*

The journey to Erin a' Fee took some time. Emer thought it might have been shorter, but after she fell off twice, having gone to sleep from sheer exhaustion, the mare took more and longer rests.

Each day, Emer conjured food for herself, as well as oatcakes for the kelpie. By the end of the first week, her stocks must have been drained. The next day the pieces were formed into different shapes. Emer always made rounded triangles. Rory had experimented with squares and circles and a rather lumpy star.

The next week's batch was even more interesting, with hearts and diamonds and a strange one she thought was a letter E.

"For me, I expect," she remarked to Fash.

It was too big to put in her mouth, so she broke it. It was as well she did, for it yielded another piece of crystal, this one shining blue.

Emer examined it, wondering why he'd sent it. It was beautiful, but an odd thing to carry on a journey. She threaded it on the wool with the first one.

By the time she finally arrived at Erin a' Fee, which she recognised by the white leprechaun villages set in a green meadow of a land, her makeshift necklace had seven crystals, all in different colours.

Fash carried her right through several villages and

eventually trotted to a dimple of a valley with a lake running along it. A turf-roofed house rested in a productive garden.

Fash stopped, raised her head and neighed imperiously.

A grey pony trotted to meet her, and they exchanged nickers and nibbled one another's manes.

Emer, perceiving she had arrived at her mother's new home, slid down and divided her latest package of oatcake between Fash and the pony.

She was weary, but there was no chance to collect her thoughts. Dornie ran out of the house and threw her arms around her daughter.

"Welcome to Rósanna Locha, dearie! That's what this village is named, for the roses by the lake. Och, why am I telling you this? You must be tired."

Emer admitted to it, but she said she had more than enough energy to kiss her mother, which she did.

Dornie ushered her into the house, where Emer reacquainted herself with her father-by-love, whose name she finally discovered was Lambert O'Shea, and met her small sister, a rosy-cheeked dumpling named Dervla Flower.

"I was planning to make a quilt for our Flower, but I put it off until you could stitch it with me," Dornie said.

Emer said, "Can we lay the first stitches today, to celebrate being together again?"

"Dearie, I was hoping ye'd say that."

Erin a' Fee was a lovesome place, and Emer was pleased to discover Dornie was a much-valued person in the village of Rósanna Locha and beyond. She wasn't the only lady of a different order, for the colleens of Erin a' Fee, just like the ones of the green way villages at home, sometimes went off to the human realm of *over there* and failed to return.

"They can *pass*," Dornie said. She smiled affectionately at Lambert, whose green skin assured Emer he would *never* pass and probably didn't want to.

The imbalance of colleens to gossoons meant the gossoons had to be *extra* loving to entice a colleen. It was so at the green way near the pixie forest and just as much so at Rósanna Locha.

"But to be sure, some of us get a better plan and find a sweet darlin' from another order," Lambert said.

With the help of a kelpie bottle.

Emer had left the bottle at home, snug in her kist.

"Flower will be able to *pass*," Dornie said, with mingled pride and regret in her tone.

"That she will, and be sure, we'll see she has her chance if she wants it."

Emer had had her own *chance* when she was fourteen, spending a year making long visits to her mother's second cousin, Kerry, a colleen who split her time between realms. She'd found plenty to interest her *over there,* in Kerry's home at *Fayhaven,* but she didn't want to live there. Indeed Kerry had spent much more time in the green way when war broke out *over there.* All was well now, and she'd returned to her human-style life where she and her husband mentored and nurtured young fay.

"Flower can go to darlin' Kerry when the time comes," Dornie said. She frowned and added, "She'll need to travel to the green way first. The gateway here heads off to London, and Kerry's not there, not by far."

"Where *is* the nearest gateway here?" Emer asked. She'd always lived near two of them, one in the pixie forest and another leading to the gateway church of St Botolph's, where Master Grene had often taken services.

"'Tis a weary way. A fishin' boat will take ye to the Isle o' Samhradh in the Star Pin, an' then it's the fair wind fleet to Heather an' on to Arrival," Lambert said.

"Heather is where you got the kelpie bottle?"

"Indade, from a lady o' the place. My godmother, she was." He smiled lovingly at Dornie and then turned to Emer.

"Ye've not used it yet for a wish?"

"No need at present. I'm happy in my life."

"No good man courtin' ye?"

"It's not time for that."

"But ye're—"

Dornie put it, "Darlin', remember, Emer has *the sight*. It tells her she'll no' wed until thirty."

He seemed nonplussed.

Dornie said gently, "You were a single man for long past then, my love."

His skin darkened in a leprechaun blush. "Your pardon, Mistress Emer."

"No need to beg my pardon. It's as well you *were* a single man until forty. Had ye not been, how could ye ha' wed Mam and made her the happiest lassie in Erin a' Fee?"

Dornie laughed at her mimicry. "I'm not even the *only* lassie in Erin a' Fee. A couple o' Heatherwomen have come to wed the fine green laddies here."

Emer was delighted to find her mother so happy in her new situation. Lambert made her welcome as his daughter-by-love and introduced her to his friends.

When Emer had explored the neighbourhood, Lambert took the whole family to visit Heather Island, a place of such bounteous beauty Emer felt quite awed by it.

She and Dornie sat in the heather with the quilt they were working between them while Lambert and his parents, who had joined the party, took Flower to look for heather gems, pieces of shining purple quartz that reminded Emer of Rory and his pisky mentor.

The quilt had a pattern of horseshoes and shamrock, but Dornie, with a mischievous smile, took up a white piece and threaded her needle with heather-coloured wool.

"That's no' part of the pattern," Emer said.

"It *will* be part of wee Flower's pattern," Dornie replied.

She breathed in the heather-scented air. "I miss the brae, dearie. I miss *you*."

"But you're happy with Lambert?" Emer said.

"That I am. But a lassie can hold two loves in her heart together."

"Lambert and dear old Da?"

"That, of course." Dornie knotted in a heather flower. She was working freehand, and she paused to check the design. "And also yourself and Flower. But in this case, I was speaking of the brae and Erin a' Fee."

"I wish you were closer, so we could visit more often," Emer said.

"So do I. But ye're here now, my lassie, and here, on this island, I have a little bit of the brae."

On another occasion, Emer cared for Flower in the cottage while Lambert and Dornie went off to a festival on Bodhran Island where Dornie later reported they had danced all day and *rested up* in the village *an Ghrá*. The twinkle in her eye suggested not much resting had occurred.

Emer loved the village. She loved Erin a' Fee, and she loved her small sister. She enjoyed the society of Lambert's parents, an elderly but spry couple named Cormac Méara Glas and Dervla Rósanna, but after a while, she felt restless. In Lambert's house, she was a welcome guest, but she had no responsibilities. Dornie's garden flourished without her needing to work in it, for Cormac, who informed her his chosen last name translated to *Greenfingers*, could, as he further informed her, grow carrots in pure salt.

"Sure, I have the touch, darlin'," he said. He looked up at her from under a broad-brimmed hat. "Now, there's that dratted pair into my cabbages again. Might ye conjure some pebbles to just miss their thievin' noses?" His smile, like his son's, informed her he was joking. He was fond of the pony, Glory-Be, and viewed the kelpie with respect and caution equally mixed.

Emer conjured some of Dornie's shamrock bread and lured Fash and her companion out of the garden. She learned that the leprechauns of Erin a' Fee, like those of the green way at home, didn't conjure.

CHAPTER EIGHT: A QUILT FOR FLOWER

1950, Rósanna Locha, Erin a' Fee

The quilt Emer and Dornie had begun to work on the day of her arrival was all but done. At first, the work had gone quickly, but after a time, it slowed. Dornie often paused, with her needle held motionless, while she recounted a story or reminisced of the times when Emer was the same age as Flower was now.

Emer knew, without conscious thought, that Dornie had an unspoken reason for taking her time at finishing the task.

Emer began to ache for her own garden, her cottage, and her own routine of making salves and ointments. Dornie made them in Rósanna Locha, but Emer perceived growing differences in their methods and recipes. Dornie's salves, fairly enough, depended on roses and clover bloom for their efficacy. Hers had more to do with forest plants that rarely grew at Erin a' Fee.

Besides, beloved daughter or not, she was a woman grown, and she wanted her own life back.

After a year and a half, she was ready to go home, but Dornie begged her to stay longer. "If you'll mind Flower, Lambert and I can sail with the fair wind fleet once more."

"Cormac and Dervla—"

Dornie smiled. "They *téigh a luí leis na cearca*, as the saying goes."

"Go to bed with the hens?" Emer hazarded. She had picked up some of the leppy dialect of Erin a' Fee during her time

36

there.

"Indeed, and our Flower sleeps only when it pleases her."

"She'll sleep better when she has her quilt to cuddle in."

That was as far as she had ever gone to suggest the job should be finished.

"I know that," Dornie said.

"I'll stay on, then, Mam, for a wee while more."

What else could she say?

Dornie took her hands. "It will put you in practice for when ye have bairns of your own."

"Your grandchildren," Emer said.

Dornie looked sad for a moment and then raised her eyes to Emer's. "Dearie, ye could always stay here with us for good and all."

"But—"

"I know, I know, the love o' your life will come when you get to thirty. I *know* that. But couldn't he come to ye here, just as well as back at the brae? There are fine men here and are they not thirsting for a lovie to hold onto forever? Have ye not noticed how many single men come to drink poteen with Lambert and his da?"

Emer had noticed. She had seen their merry eyes light up at the sight of her and heard their soft voices greeting her as she went about her business. She had danced with them at the *Paddy Cèilidh* to familiar tunes as well as some that were indigenous to Erin a' Fee. She liked them all very well, but she was careful never to favour one over the others. It would not be fair. As with the braw laddies of the brae, she had no more to offer them than a hand of friendship.

She sidestepped that thorny subject. "Och, Mam, I don't live at the brae now. You ken fine I have my cottage at the edge of the pixie forest. That's where Fash found me, and the dear Lord knows how she did. Maybe that was why she was so out of charity cross when she came to me. She might have been waiting up the brae for a wee while. That's where I have to be, though, at my cottage. That's where the love of my life will come to me."

Dornie turned away to gaze unseeingly across her garden, where Cormac, her father-by-love, tended to hilling up the tatties, stopping now and again to talk to the pony, Glory-Be. Then, after a bit, she turned back to Emer and smiled. She said cheerfully, "That's that then, dearie. I'll say no more on that . . . ever."

"I'm sorry, Mam."

"No need to be sorry! How could I keep you from the love of a good man, when I've been blessed wid that twice over?"

Emer managed a smile, for Dornie had assumed a strong leppy lilt.

"I hope to be as blessed as you, though, I think I'd prefer to be blessed just once."

"In that case, lassie, best be choosing a younger laddie than I did first off. I loved my Davey-laddie so dearly, but he was well and truly more than my age now when he brought me to the cottage as his bride. He'd lost his Sorcha-Mary and mourned her for much too long before he looked about him again. So, choose a younger laddie than I did, if the choice is down to you."

"Perhaps I will," Emer said. She reflected that she knew nothing at all about her father's first bride, except that she had been an older lassie, past the age for bearing children when they wed.

I should have asked Da about her. He loved her, and there's no one left to mourn for her now.

"Mam, did you ever know Sorcha-Mary?"

Dornie shook her head. "No, lassie. At least—not to say *know her*. I saw her about, and we were of *greet you, mistress,* terms, but she was an old lassie to me. I was maybe Flower's age when she went to glory."

"So you knew Da then?"

"I did. He and my da were friends, though my Davey was older." She smiled down at her hands, and Emer saw the flash of the ring from her first marriage, which she wore now on her right hand. "My da, your grandad, Emer, was a dear man. I wish you could have known him."

"So do I," Emer said.

"When he passed on, just a wee time after Mam, Davey came to me. He said it should have been him that passed and he told me to come to him if ever I was in need of fatherly advice. He had no bairns of his own, but he said he would do his best."

"Did you ever?" Emer asked.

Dornie turned the ring on her finger. "I said I had no need of fatherly advice just then, but I hugged him and kissed him on the cheek and thanked him kindly. He said it was the first hug and kiss he'd had since his Sorcha-Mary passed, and I said to him to come to me if he was ever in need of another."

"So I suppose he did."

"Aye, after a while. It was fun between us, you see. He'd come with a piece of advice, and I'd pay him with a hug and a kiss. Or sometimes, I'd give him a hug and a kiss, and he'd give me a piece of advice. Oh, some of them were that funny! After the first few months, they got funnier every time. I found I needed advice quite often." She smiled and added, "He was a dear laddie, and we had many a laugh, and all our years together were happy ones."

"He was a dear," Emer said.

"Aye, you look like him—pure Drumwiddy."

"Along with *the sight and all*," Emer said drily.

"*The sight.*" Dornie sighed. "So, ye have to go, but ye'll stay for just a wee while longer?"

"I will. I'll stay until Flower's quilt is done."

"Let that be, then. And I promise I won't drag my heels on the stitching from now on."

"Have you been doing that?"

"You know fine I have! Not that I knew it until now. I deluded myself I wanted to make it perfect. Dearie, do not delude yourself. Try to know your reason for doing . . . or not doing . . . things. It will save you a mighty load of trouble."

Dornie and Lambert *took the fleet* as Lambert put it, a week later. They went to Bodhran Island and spent a month living alone there in the white village, but for passing visitors.

Emer and Flower had the cottage to themselves, though Cormac and Dervla came by as usual.

Emer explained to Flower that she would soon be going home.

The little girl's lip trembled. "I'll never see ye anymore!"

"Oh, but you will, darlin'! I might visit again, and when you're a bigger maid, maybe ye'll come to me in my cottage and meet the red cat!"

"Is the red cat lonely while ye're gone?"

"I hope not." Emer knew he was.

If he'd been a natural cat, it would have been unpardonable to leave him alone for so long. Luckily, Rory had his guardians and his lessons at the castle. No doubt, too, he was still visiting the pisky jeweller and his wife.

"Shall we send the red cat a message?" she said brightly.

Flower nodded. She drew a picture of herself and Emer and wrote their names in careful letters.

"Now then, we'll conjure that back to my cottage and see if he finds it."

"Can the red cat read?" The child sounded doubtful.

"Sure, he can! He's a special cat, a *cat draíochta*." She brought out the leprechaun term with pride.

Flower said, "Just like Fash. Sure, she's a *capal draíochta*. Glory-Be is a *capal*, just."

"Hush, dearie. Don't let Glory-Be hear you saying that."

"Sure, he won't mind. He knows what he is, and he's happy in his hide," Flower said brightly.

Rory's not quite like Fash, Emer thought. As far as she was aware, the cranky mare had only one form.

Emer conjured the drawing and a message from herself back to her cottage. She cautioned Flower that the red cat would not reply.

"He has never been to Erin a' Fee, and so he can't conjure here. He may not even go to my cottage anymore."

She felt melancholy at the thought, but the idea that Rory *did* still go to the cottage was even worse.

Two days later, on a whim, she tried to conjure oatcake from her kitchen crock.

Not that it will be fit to eat after this long while.

To her surprise, a batch popped out of the air, crock and all.

It will be mouldy.

It wasn't. It was fresh and sweet, made in elegant hearts and stars.

He's coming on!

She was amused and touched to discover he'd sent a tiny wooden carving of a cat with amber crystal eyes.

For Flower?

She knew it was for her.

An oatcake in a big letter F had a flower carving set with a sparkling red stone.

So, he goes to the cottage still.

She conjured back a message.

Dear Rory . . . I'm coming home.

CHAPTER NINE: THE REUNION

1950, The Pixie Forest, Over There

Farewelling the family at Erin a' Fee was tearful, but Emer knew she'd see them again. In a few years, Flower would need to be sponsored *over there*. Emer would take her to the gateway in the pixie forest and see her safely to Cousin Kerry.

The thought made her nervous. It was years since she'd been *over there*. Maybe Kerry would come to the forest to fetch her.

No. I'll take Flower myself. I'll visit her, too, somehow.

The sight showed her that would be so, flashing a picture of what was, unmistakably, the lighthouse at Shipley, the town nearest Kerry's welcoming home. It failed to show Flower or herself, though there was a woman in a wide-skirted human-style dress which blew around her legs. That was Shipley Light, though, and what other reason could Emer have for being there?

On the last morning, Emer and Dornie sat down with the quilt between them. Dornie picked up her needle and then put it down with a sigh. "It's done, dearie. No use pretending it's not."

"Here, though." Emer threaded up a heather-coloured wool and stitched a neat capital E into the last patch she'd done. She threaded up shamrock green and over-stitched part of the E, so it became an F as well.

"Will you put a heart around it?" Dornie asked.

Emer shook her head. "That's for Flower to do later, if she

remembers me fondly, and if she chooses. My part is done." She laid down the needle and pulled Dornie to her feet. They held one another in a long hug.

Fash, the kelpie, carried her home. Lambert had said she might cut the journey short by travelling with the fair wind fleet, but Emer wanted the time to reflect. She wanted to transition from herself-as-beloved-guest-and-daughter back to herself-as-mistress-of-her-life.

She'd let Rory know she was coming, and soon the pattern of conjuring oatcakes began again. Some of them were capital Es, and these were often housing crystals. Emer's necklace was full, so she made herself a bracelet to match.

Fash was almost agreeable and seemed to hurry the last few miles.

Emer watched the familiar country shift around her. She got Fash to stop at her mother's cottage, expecting to find it in need of repair.

It was as clean and bright as during Dornie's tenure. The garden brimmed with produce.

Emer slept in her old bed while Fash made free with the salads in the garden, unhindered by Cormac Méara Glas.

The next day they were off again, moving swiftly until Emer saw her own beloved cottage dreaming in the sun.

The garden glowed with wellbeing. Her little pine tree had grown breast-high.

Emer slid off Fash's back for the last time . . . for now. She stroked the kelpie's mane and dared to kiss her soft nose. "Thank you, dearie. You carried me well."

Fash tossed her head and transferred her attention to someone behind Emer.

Emer turned and saw a handsome red cat squatting on its haunches, licking a paw.

"Red?"

He'd grown into his skin. No suggestion of the kitten remained.

Emer picked him up and hugged him. He purred, rubbing his cheek against her bosom.

Fash snorted.

Emer put the red cat down and watched as it communed with the kelpie.

"I'll leave you two to say your pieces," she said and walked wearily into the cottage.

She found the kettle boiling and unmistakable signs of long-term habitation.

So Rory had taken her at her word. He'd kept the cottage warm and fitting. He'd been working in the garden, too.

Emer poured a cup of tea for herself and made one for Rory.

Where *was* the laddie? Surely he wasn't still communing with the mare?

A slab of oatcake by the tea caddy vanished.

Ah, he's gifting Fash. Must be in lad form.

She was about to draw the curtains to see when she heard a tap on the door.

She called, "Bit superfluous to tap on a door where you've been living, wee laddie."

The door opened, and a man's voice said, "*Wee laddie* indeed! What about our rules, Emer?"

She turned to face her young friend.

"You've grown."

"You haven't."

"Well, no, I stopped growing years ago."

She held out her hand, tilting her head up to meet his amber gaze. "Rory, how can I thank you for keeping the cottage so well? And the garden, and Mam's cottage . . . och, you're such a treasure."

"I was happy to do it."

His gaze moved to her neck and wrist and lit on the crystal

jewellery. "You liked the wee gifts?"

"You can see I did. I'm draped with jewels and dripping with gems."

He came closer, bent and kissed her cheek, and then closed his arms around her in a hug. "Welcome home, my queen."

She laughed and hugged him back, smelling the familiar scent of incense that hung about him and the red cat. She stepped back. "So, you must be what — sixteen already?"

He grinned and ducked his head, and she saw a flash of the little lad he'd been. "Seventeen come summer."

"And that's when I'll be twenty-nine." She sighed and felt an odd twinge of *the sight*. She put it away. "We might celebrate together," she said.

"We shall. I have plans."

"Oh, have ye indeed, *balach gràdhach*? What are those? A major baking session?"

"You'll see, *mo bhean*."

She hugged him again. "Och, ye wee besom, ye'll be talkin' like a true braesider soon. It's so good to be home! I'll need to conjure a note to Flower. She wanted me to send her reports of the red cat."

"I'll drink my tea, and then you can have him in the flesh and send an accurate report," he said. He kissed her brow and stepped away quickly to take up his tea.

Emer thought Rory must have been living in the cottage to have kept it in such good heart, but after their tea, he said goodbye and went off to his guardians' house.

Sure, and they'll be surprised to see him, she thought.

Och, better watch for that. I've got Erin a' Fee on my tongue, just like Mam.

She settled contentedly back to her old life, visited often by the red cat. Rory still drank tea with her in lad form, but he spent a disproportionate amount of time in his furry self. Red was a handsome cat and very affectionate. He liked to sleep on Emer's lap or drape himself around her shoulders, purring all the while.

Sometimes she wondered if he might one day choose to be a full-time cat. Mutable fay with animal manifests occasionally did so. One day, in early December, she had a chance to find out more.

CHAPTER TEN: MASTER FLOPPY

December 1951, *The Pixie Forest, Over There*

At first, Emer thought she and the pisky jeweller met by chance when he came to the pixie forest to deliver a gift.

Emer was out collecting kindling when she saw a roan spaniel dog trotting purposefully along the path with a cloth pouch dangling from its jaws.

"Now, where are you going with that, my friend?" She paused to watch, caught in a memory.

Rory drew you . . . that day by the stove.

She still had that sketch of the spaniel and the distant woman. It was in the kist, and she should have given it back to Rory, although he'd probably forgotten its existence. He still sketched, now and then, though he never showed her his work.

The dog paused, waving its plume of a tail.

Emer shook off the memory and offered a small square of oatcake conjured from her crock. Fay dogs weren't especially common, but they, like the fay goats and the chalklands hill ponies, always appreciated a treat.

The spaniel put down the pouch, lifted its head and unfolded into a spare man with pointed ears and brilliant hazel eyes. He wore pixie britches and a tunic crisscrossed with so many silver bindings strung with crystals that Emer was dazzled. He had fair hair going grey and a short silver earring in one ear.

He laughed at her surprise. "Greet you, mistress, and thank

you for the gift."

Emer recovered her self-possession, trying not to blush at her mistake. "There's a cup of tea with it, if you want, master."

"I'll say yes. Mind, I'm not looking for a lassie to bed. I have a fine pisky minx at home." He touched his earring. "Thirty-odd years we've had together and look forward to a lot more still."

"*No harm,*" she assured him, amused. "I'm just on my way home."

"Jago Pendennis," he said when they reached the cottage. *Ah.* "Emer Drumwiddy."

He gave her a more appraising look. "You'll be Rory's queen, then."

"And I expect you'll be the red cat's friend who likes oat-cakes." *And who once had his portrait drawn in my kitchen.*

"I am. And now I see why the boy wanted all those crystals. They become you, Rory's Queen. They bring out the colour in your beautiful brae eyes."

"Call me Emer. I have no idea why Rory refers to me as *queen.*"

"Have you not?"

Emer put tea in the pot. "No. In fact, I have very little idea of why Rory does anything. The red cat is much easier to understand. He's very direct. Cats usually are."

"A bold creature. He tried to whisker wipe my minx one time. I soon put paid to that. Chased him up a tree."

"You did not."

"Threatened to. In the end, I didn't have to. My minx sorted it out." He sniffed. "Can't say I blame the poor beast. Emblyn smells of cat-nip. Makes Master Floppy sneeze when it's going to storm."

"Dare I ask who Master Floppy is?"

"Who d'you think? I'll have you know *no* part of me is floppy when it needs to be otherwise. Ask my minx. Or don't.

She might sort *you* out." He sighed happily. "Master Floppy is the spaniel. Referring to his ears, you know. Pisky ears are important, even when they're floppy and covered with roan fur. My minx understands that."

Emer poured water on the tea and conjured oatcakes and soda bread with bramble jelly.

"You're quiet," the pisky man said.

"Mm."

"What is it that you want to ask me?"

"Is it that obvious?"

She turned to look at him and blinked again at the dazzle of silver and gems. "Does your miss wear as much silver as you?"

"More. And she's a minx. Some pisky gals are misses, like the pixies. Mine is a minx. We have a couple of near-grown misses, Chesten and Penzance, Emblyn's big boy Enyon who's a man grown and mostly working with his dad, and our boy Truro, a few years younger than Rory. Already teaching him his decent pisky manners. Tried with Rory, too, but it's awkward. I can teach him mutie manners, but not how to be a decent pisky man. He's not one, and so it would never *take*." He rubbed his chin. "Blessed if I know *what* Rory is, aside from a mutie. More orders to his blood than anyone knows, I'd say. No harm in that, mind," he added, possibly perceiving that Emer herself had a drop of leprechaun blood in her makeup.

"None at all," she said equably. "I'm glad he has you to advise him, though. I did not know his family. He's mentioned only one fairly distant cousin, but I think Red—the red cat—was a surprise to him as well as to his guardians."

"Would have got the mutie gene from his ma, and maybe his da, too . . . whoever he was. You never met Annie Inkersoll?"

"I don't think so. I don't know the name."

He laughed. "Rory's ma. Lovely maid, so I hear, but she had him late and . . . well, sad tale. Never tell me you don't know his last name?"

Emer raised her eyebrow. "You know . . . I didn't. I never asked, and he never told me."

"And old Berryman wouldn't tell you what the boy hadn't."

"I don't see much of the Grenes. I used to go to services with Mam and Da now and then, but not often since Da went to glory."

"Not long 'til the boy takes over. Reverend Rory Inkersoll. Quite a ring to it."

He raised a brow, mimicking Emer. "You didn't know that."

"I did not." She added, with a burst of displeasure, "And you needn't have told me. Rory tells me what he wants me to know."

"Not all, I'll warrant." He ate a piece of oatcake. "So, what did you want to ask me? I know it wasn't about my silver or my family. Ask away, whatever it is. It'll go no farther."

Emer stared at her bracelet. There were so many things she wanted to know, but she felt she shouldn't go behind Rory's back.

The pisky said, "Want to know how lovies of muties work the bedding without getting clawed?"

What! Emer felt a hot blush rushing over her face and chest. She was speechless.

"Not that? Well, I'll tell you anyway. My Emblyn, the delight of my loins, the minx of my heart, wanted to know that before we said *forever*. Can't say I blame her. *I* couldn't tell her, not being what you might call an experienced man. Lucky my grandad, Tintagel, was a mutie, too."

"So you asked him?" Emer tried to visualise that conversation.

"I did not. My minx went along to visit Granny Dem . . . Demela Pendennis, she was, fine old miss. Sat down over tea and a nice hevva cake. Talked the matter out. Saved my blushes." He smiled, shaking his head. "I'd have given a cream tea to have been present at *that* conversation."

"Obviously it worked out for you," Emer ventured.

"Lord, yes! Granny Dem gave it to my minx straight-about. *The dog is not the man, and the man is not the dog.* True, that. Master Floppy's fond of Emblyn. He licks her hand and snuggles in her lap. He'd defend her and love her to the last breath, but to him, she's his friend. A cuddle friend. He'd no more want to service her than a stag would lust for a she-cat. Mind, I'm a licker, too. My minx doesn't mind *that*."

He smiled faintly. "So I've shocked you, Mistress Emer. But you need to know. You can be as loving as you feel to the red cat. He'll love you right back, but it'll be purry, rub-the-whiskers and knead-the-knees . . . nothing more. Mind, he might try to put his mark on you."

"Might he, now."

"The whisker wipe. That's why my minx set him skit-scat. Master Floppy is the only furry friend who can claim *her*, and so she told him. He tried to stare her down, but *nobody* stares my minx down. Not even me." He fixed his bright eyes, curious but kind, on Emer's. "So, does our red friend claim you?"

Emer remembered a few things. "He does. He started when he was a kitten."

"Bonded to you, then. That's fine, but it could get complicated, for all that. You're not wed, mistress?"

"No! Not likely to be either, until . . ."

"Until?"

She shrugged. "I have *the sight*. It's fickle, but a few things are plain. I knew the red cat would come. And I know that eight years on my true love will come. I can't look for him until I'm thirty."

"How old now?"

"Twenty-nine this summer."

"Hm. That is definitely complicated. When this man of yours gets his arse into your chair and his cock in your bed, then the red cat will be a mite put out. He'll see the attention and caresses he's claimed as *his* going to some stranger."

"I'd never reject Red. I promised him that."

"But what of our Rory when your man comes?"

"By then, he'll be off courting, and—when does he get his calling?"

"Master Grene says a bishop will see him when he's twenty-one. Not before. Won't be the current man . . . Father Baskerton that is, since he's older than any man has a right to be."

"Rory will be studying hard until then."

"Bless you, mistress. He knows the good book back and forth already. What's more, he holds it in here." He tapped his chest. "He'll be a fine pastor for the forest and for St Botolph's, too."

"That won't stop him from going courting."

She thought briefly of the halfling girl he'd once mentioned. What was her name . . . Gia? As the result of an unlikely union between a tree lad and a courtfolk lady, she, too, might be difficult to categorise. Treefolk were affectionate, so she might be delighted to cradle Red in her arms. Rory, too.

Jago Pendennis grimaced and drained his tea. "You're right. He'll be courting, and maybe sooner than you think. And now I'll be off home."

"What about your package?"

"My—" He slapped one of his many pockets. "Left it outside." He flicked his fingers and conjured the cloth pouch to the table. "You can open it. Might be a bit of dog spit on it, but no harm in that."

"You mean, it's for me?"

"Of course, it is. A gift from your friend and mine. It wasn't by chance that we met out there on the path."

Emer took the pouch. "Why didn't he bring it to me himself?"

The pisky lifted a shoulder. "Could be, the lad's busy. Could be, he thought you might have questions you hesitated to put to him. When I said I saw to his mutie education, I meant that literally. I told him the facts. Told him to stay away from she-cats when they're calling. *He* won't be bothered, but the fay toms will. They can be right nasty when roused. The red cat won't fight for himself, though he might for whoever Rory loves. He could get badly hurt if he didn't know the facts."

Emer winced. "What would happen if Red was hurt? Would Rory be hurt, too?"

"Now, that's a question and a half. I'll have to say no . . . or, not in the normal way. I mean, if a fat tom got him a lucky bite on the scruff, Rory wouldn't be bleeding, or even bruised, in man-form. He'd suffer, though. If his cat's hurt, he'll feel *wrong*. That's the only way to put it."

"Wrong," Emer repeated.

"One time, Master Floppy got a kick from one of the ponies up on the chalk. The beast didn't mean it. It was a case of parallel paths that suddenly weren't so parallel. Next thing I knew, I was flat on the chalk, man-form, feeling as if the world had ended and me with it. A little boy found me and yelled *Ma!* The most glorious minx that ever wore silver bent over me and told me to get up and stop maundering because I was scaring her boy." He tugged absently at his earring.

"Never saw anything I wanted so much as I wanted that minx, but I felt too bad to so much as offer to kiss her ear. Mind, that would have been a bad idea, since I was not much past sixteen and she was twenty-so. But that's old news. I grew up, and she came to look at me with more favour. Once

Master Floppy recovered from that kick, *he* went to work on our minx. Couldn't resist *him* for long. Nothing can look more forlorn than a spaniel that's not getting his fair share of attention." He smiled wickedly.

"But getting back to mutie education, let's just say I've done my best for our Rory *and* for his cat."

Emer fastened on the one thing that bothered her in all this. "Did Rory send you to talk to me?"

"No, mistress. He asked me to bring your gift. The rest, I took upon myself."

"That was good of you."

"Not offended then?"

"No. Grateful." She loosened the ties on the pouch and extracted the contents. "Oh."

"Not so bad for his first attempt," the pisky said.

Emer turned the trinket about, running her fingers over its surface.

"Red marble. Easier to carve than quartz, but still needs a lot of time. The eyes are ambers."

"It's lovely. Did you teach him this?"

"Taught him the techniques. But the form and the heart of the piece comes from *him*. Could be he didn't know what it would be when he began. I often don't."

Emer set the marble cat on the dresser. It glowed with an inner warmth and reflected the fire in the stove.

The pisky man got up, took back the pouch and said his farewells. She escorted him back to the path.

Just before he left, he smiled at her and said, "See how long it is 'til you have to go and stroke it again."

"It's an ornament."

"And you think our fine young man hasn't slipped a charm or two into the making? Priest-in-waiting, he is. Saint, he's not." He dropped the pouch on the ground and melted into the spaniel dog, which picked up the pouch in its jaws.

"Thank you, Master Floppy. Watch out for not-so-parallel ponies," Emer said.

The dog gave her a merry look from hazel pisky eyes and trotted off.

CHAPTER ELEVEN: SEVEN YEARS ON

December 10, 1951, *The Pixie Forest, Over There*

Emer's twenty-ninth birthday brought her much to think about.

In one more year she could look for her lover-to-be.

For just one year more, she and Rory would be free to pursue their friendship unhindered by consideration of anyone else.

Their birthdays, as she discovered with a fatalistic touch of *the sight*, fell on the same day.

She'd never known exactly when his was, but she knew she should have realised. He was always melancholy around that time.

Thinking of his mother, poor laddie.

She sometimes wondered about Annie Inkersoll. She had written to Dornie, who had replied to say she knew the name, but could not remember the bearer. The Grenes presumably knew much more, but Emer didn't want to pry. For the same reason, she didn't ask Rory about his mother. She thought he'd tell her if he ever wanted her to know.

She made him a gift for his birthday, a clerical collar embroidered with braeside wool from the McTavish flock in the braelands. Cromarty McTavish was a distant connection of her father, and he was happy to supply her with wool as red as fay sheep ever got.

She sewed slowly and put in a charm of safety.

When Rory arrived on his birthday and hers, spruced up

in a new linen shirt from his guardians, her heart caught at how handsome he'd become.

"Happy birthday, wee laddie."

He laughed and came for a hug. "Less of the *wee*, my queen."

She said, "Seventeen!"

"Yes. Seven years we've been together."

"Not exactly that."

"No. You left me for a good, long, while."

"Did I ever thank you for looking after my cottage and Mam's?"

"You did, more than once. Did I ever thank *you* for giving me a place where I could be myself and dream of you while you were gone?"

"Frequently." She conjured his gift, tied up in a scrap of Drumwiddy plaid.

He took it, smiling. "A collar for the red cat?"

"No—for you."

"I—" He undid the plaid and extracted the collar. His face drained and then flushed.

"I hope it's not inappropriate, since you're not ordained yet."

He recovered himself. "No . . . he told you, then? Master Grene?"

"Master Pendennis mentioned it."

"The old dog."

"He thought I knew."

"He did not. But never mind, I expect he meant it kindly."

He held up the collar. "Put it on for me?"

"Can you wear it yet?"

"Yes. Master Grene says I'm ready. Not officially, but ready in my heart."

She took the collar and said, "Bend down, you great tall laddie."

He motioned her to her rocking chair and kneeled at her feet, looking up at her. "This was us seven years ago."

"Only you were a good deal smaller. And naked."

He laughed. "I was that mortified."

"You had no need to be — ever."

"I won't be next time."

"There shouldn't be a next time, as long as Red doesn't fall off my lap again." She leaned forward and put on the collar.

He sighed. "It's charmed. Thank you."

"Only with a little kindness from the universe. I hope it's not inappropriate."

"Not a bit. Master Grene says there are more things in heaven and earth . . . and *over here,* too. How do I look?"

"Very handsome. Very appropriate."

"Do you have a kiss for a handsome and appropriate man?"

She kissed his cheek.

"Now, for you."

He felt in the breast of his shirt and pulled out two chains with a ring threaded on each. "These are kissing rings. One is for you and one for me."

"Rory —"

"No, don't say anything. Listen to me. I'm not asking for anything you don't feel willing to give. All I'm asking is that you wear mine over your heart. I'll wear yours the same way. If — and I know it's *if* — you ever want to put yours on your finger, then tell me. If you never do, then you can put it by, or wear it as a necklace. I'm afraid you can't give it to another man . . . but then you probably wouldn't need to. He'd be of age."

He went on gazing at her.

"Oh, Rory."

"Don't say anything final now. Just remember *if* you want a kissing ring commitment with me, you have only to say so."

Emer's heart lurched.

"What is it you want to say? Aside from *no* or *not yet*?"

She said, "You know I have *the sight*."

"Yes, of course. You knew you'd be riding to Erin a' Fee. And the day you met Red, you said something about him being here at last. I don't really know what it means."

"The red cat was the harbinger. The precursor. Eight years on, I'll meet the man I'm destined to be with all my life."

"And now it's seven years on from that day."

"Yes. So you see, I haven't met him yet."

He gave her a brilliant smile. "Of course you haven't."

"But when I do . . . you do see, laddie . . ."

How can I say it? How can I see that smile fall away?

The pisky man's words mocked her . . . and so did her own reply.

When this man of yours gets his arse into your chair and his cock in your bed, then the red cat will be a mite put out . . . what of our Rory?

He's a lad. He'll be courting by then . . .

Rory said, "When you meet your man, that'll be the day you turn thirty."

"It might not be exactly that day."

"It will be *exactly* that day. Because that's the day I'll have my eighteenth birthday. I'll have enough years to be a man." His eyes brightened. "Your man, forever. Think of it."

She thought of it. And then she started to laugh.

Chapter Twelve: Kissing Rings

December 10, 1951, *The Pixie Forest cottage, Over There*

"Funny, am I?" Rory said.

Emer wiped her eyes. "No, my darling lad, you're not. I'm laughing at myself."

"Did you know you can have a kissing ring commitment at sixteen?"

"I did not. I know nothing about them. How do *you* know?"

"Master Pendennis told me they're for folk who are wish-matched or in love, when one or both of them don't have enough years for bedding. The reason he knows is that when he met Mistress Emblyn, she was twenty-one and she had a boy already. It was arranged, you see. Master Ruan Weir wanted a son but he . . . well, Mistress Emblyn was a good friend of his family. She never wanted to wed him, but she was happy to service his wish. She likes Master Weir. He told her he couldn't wed a maid, but he would dearly love a child.

"Master Jago met her up on the chalk when he was younger than I am. He made kissing rings, one for her and one for him and luckily she agreed to wait for him to have enough years."

"How do they work?" Emer left aside the complex matter of Master Weir and his son with Mistress Emblyn. No doubt there had been a good reason for it. And if Master Jago Pendennis would rather Rory kept quiet about his family, then he should have prepaid the compliment. Come to that, he'd mentioned his Emblyn's *big boy* himself.

Rory said, "You charm them, and put in all the things you want to have happen . . . all the things that can appropriately happen. Then you can relax and know you won't go wrong. *No harm.*"

"I see." She looked into his amber eyes and felt warmth in her cheeks.

This is . . .

No, do not be ridiculous, Emer Drumwiddy.

For a moment she thought she heard Dornie's voice in her mind. *Dearie, do not delude yourself.*

All right, Mam, so I won't.

This is not ridiculous. This is right.

He laid the chain with the bigger ring on her lap. "If you'd like to put this over your head, the chain's long enough. You could also just hang it in the window so it catches the sun. I asked Master Pendennis to make it so it could be an ornament, too."

She looked down at the ring. It was a wide hoop of copper with a couple of ambers set together. "This one is yours?"

He nodded.

"May I see the other?"

He laid the other chain beside the first. This one was gold, with a fine band of mother-of-pearl running through the centre.

"No amber?"

He smiled nervously. "Look inside."

She looked at the inner surface. "I see."

"Mine has mother-of-pearl inside."

Emer picked up the larger ring and kissed it. Then she dropped the chain over her head and let the ring fall down beneath her collar.

Rory caught his breath and reached for hers.

Emer shook her head. "You've already worn this over your heart. I want this on my finger."

"But—"

She lifted his chain off her neck and said, "I wore it for a little while. Will that do?"

He nodded. "I need yours to charm."

She unclasped the chain and passed the ring to him. Then she unthreaded his. "How do we do this?"

"You put in on your finger and think about all the things we might do . . . all the appropriate things."

Emer reflected that she knew very little of such things, but she nodded and slipped his ring on her finger. He put hers on his little finger, which was the only one it would fit.

They folded their hands around the rings and sat in silence for a few minutes. Rory raised his head. "Ready?"

She smiled. "Are you sure, Rory? You really should be thinking of maids your own age."

"I have thought of them. They're not right for me. They're not *you*."

She took his left hand.

"Right hand," he murmured.

She took that and slid the ring into place.

He did the same with hers.

He got to his feet. His face shifted, and his amber eyes welled with tears. His mouth went crooked, and a broken sob came out. Emer watched him fold into the red cat.

She held out her arms. "Come on, Red. Let's snuggle."

The cat sprang into her lap and rubbed his whiskers along her hand.

"Oh, really? You're trying that *now*?" She hugged him, lifting him against her breast where he pushed his head against her and started to purr.

She held him for a while and felt him relax into sleep. "Poor wee mannie."

She sighed as she felt the weight of him in her arms. "Not so wee. You're a fine figure of a cat, Red."

She went on holding him until she was almost asleep herself. When he stirred, she gave him a final hug and leaned down to set him on the ground. She could only imagine poor Rory's embarrassment if he woke to find himself, almost a man grown, sprawled in a woman's lap.

She left her hand on him as he sighed and stretched, shifting into the young man she knew, clothed in pixie pants, his new shirt and his embroidered collar.

He blinked and put his hand to his chest, rubbing the shirt. "I did it!"

"Did what?"

He sat up. "Came back dressed. I've been practising, so I'd not need to go into the tub room every time. Master Pendennis explained how."

"I suppose he'd know." She remembered the spaniel unfolding into the pisky man. He'd been fully clad.

And just as well. A naked pisky in front of me would have been —

"I'm sorry about *that*." He got to his feet. "I'd braced myself for you to say *no*, or *maybe one day*, you see. I never thought you'd say yes. Not yet."

"It's done now, so I hope you meant it."

"I've never meant anything more." He held out his hands. "Emer . . . can we?"

She took them and let him draw her out of the chair. She moved up and stood toe to toe with him.

He released her hands and put his arms around her. They'd stood like that before, though not for a while. She rested her head on his shoulder. "Incense."

"Mm." He inhaled. "Oatcake. I've always loved the smell. While you were away, I just kept baking it, so I felt as if you were still here."

He stroked her hair. "I don't know how this will go. I've imagined it, but I haven't done it."

"I have." She smiled, remembering.

"Oh?"

"I kissed fourteen braw laddies who helped to make this cottage. It was a kiss of friendship for each, but a proper kiss. I couldn't fob them off with a buss on the cheek."

"You've done that to me."

"You were a young laddie."

"I still am."

"You don't sound like one."

He didn't feel like one, either. She moved her hands down to caress his back, feeling flat planes and ridges of muscle. "You're going to be a beautiful man, Rory Inkersoll."

He chuckled. "So you know that, too. It's Mum's name, not my father's. She never told me that. She probably didn't know."

"I couldn't believe I didn't know your other name all these years."

"You always gave me my own thoughts, my queen. You never tried to find out what I didn't want to tell."

"I never will."

"But sometimes I'd like a little encouragement . . . I would have told you my name and my calling."

"Your calling. Do you think the Lord approves of *this*?" She leaned in closer, hearing his heartbeat quicken.

"I'm sure he does. He's full of love. So is this."

"So is this." She lifted her head from his shoulder and raised her face to his. "Rory Inkersoll, are you going to kiss me, or shall we stand here all day?"

"I'm going to kiss you. If I have to be the red cat afterwards . . . please understand."

"I will."

He brought his lips to hers, and they touched. He was definitely unpractised, but Emer let him take the lead. He lifted away and gasped and then moved in again, holding her tightly against him.

Emer's mind anxiously told her this wasn't right, or fair.

She bade it sharply to be silent. Her body said this was fine, but it wanted a lot more than an unpractised lad. She snapped at it to behave. He pressed against her and started to tremble.

She drew her face back and tucked it into his shoulder, stroking his back. "It's all right, Rory. You can be the red cat if you need to."

He drew a shuddering breath. "No. I want to be me. I want to go on holding you and kissing you but . . . I didn't know it would be so *hard*."

"I'm hard to kiss?" She tried to sound arch and teasing.

"No! You're wonderful. Everything I imagined. I meant so hard not to want —"

"Not to want what we didn't put in the kissing rings." She relaxed against him. "I think you could probably just let it go if you need to."

He stepped back. "Certainly not! I will *not* do that."

"Maybe we'd better not do *this* then."

"We will do this. A lot. Often. I'll learn to be better at it."

She held out her arms and hugged him, shaking with giggles. "Don't get too much better, or I'll be the one letting go, and then you'll have to deal with the yelping."

"The *yelping*?"

She bit her lip. "My friend Catriona is wed to Master Chaucer. She informs me there is yelping. There are also the occasional squeaks and squelches and some incomprehensible babble and the occasional unintended giggle."

"I will not yelp."

"I might."

"No." He looked affronted.

"Rory, I might. I might do all sorts of things. So might you. That is perfectly fine."

"But not now."

"Certainly not now." She raised her face and kissed his lower lip.

65

He turned them about and sat down abruptly in the rocking chair, pulling her into his lap. "Let's practise. But if I do anything inappropriate . . ."

"I'll yelp."

"You will not." He kissed her, catching her lip gently in his teeth. She squirmed. He was a quick learner.

It was going to be a long year.

Chapter Thirteen: Old Before You

1952, *The Pixie Forest, Over There*

It was a long year for Emer and also a delightful one. They kissed a lot, breaking off when it became uncomfortable. Emer still wasn't sure how the kissing rings worked, but she supposed they helped to bring things to a halt when necessary.

Otherwise, they went on as usual, baking, gardening, and gathering ingredients for Emer's salves in the pixie forest. Sometimes they tended the garden at Dornie's house, although Emer increasingly wondered why. Dornie was never coming back to live there.

She heard from the family at Erin a' Fee often. Since both sides had been to visit the others, Emer and Dornie could now conjure back and forth. Lambert, as with most leprechaun gossoons, did not conjure. Emer wasn't sure if the leppy men couldn't do it or simply didn't. Maybe one day, she'd ask Lambert.

In one exchange of notes, Emer asked Dornie what she should do about the cottage.

Dearie, I'd like fine if you would keep it on a while. We might visit soon and again when Flower needs to go over there.

That made sense. With Rory spending so much time with her, the work of caring for both cottages and gardens was easy.

"I hope you're keeping up with your studies with Master Grene." She tried to sound matter-of-fact instead of admonitory. This year of the kissing ring must also, she knew, be a year of transition from friendship between a woman and a lad to a love-relationship between equals.

"I am."

"And your studies with Master Pendennis."

"I don't need that so much now. The red cat is grown up."

"He certainly is. He has a lordly tomcat nose now. As have you." She tapped his nose with a floury finger.

Rory caught her hand and kissed it, and then dusted off the flour. "Emer, you won't need to worry about the red cat when we bed together. He'll be asleep."

"Does he sleep when we're kissing?"

"Mm."

"You don't sound certain.

"He just purrs away in a dream. He knows you and I are loving one another. He loves you, too, and he's happy."

He rubbed his cheek against her shoulder and kissed her neck, gaining more flour in the process.

Emer shivered. They were close to their birthdays.

"All right, my queen?" He lifted his head.

"Yes. I think the kissing rings are losing their grip."

"They will be. They should be. They need to be. Otherwise, they'd stop us when we *can*."

"Will you stay with me some nights then?"

He held her back and gave her a stern look. "After we're wed, I'll be here every night neither of us is needed elsewhere."

"We're to be wed, then?"

"Didn't you know?"

"I thought so, but not until you're a bit older."

"Why wait? I'm going to be with you for the rest of my life."

"The rest of *my* life, darling Rory."

"My life." His stubborn chin came out.

"No. From what you told me before, you may have some sylvan blood. You could live a very long time. In any case, I'm going to be old before you."

He pulled her hard against him. "You're not to leave me. I couldn't bear it. I won't bear it. If you go to glory, I'm coming with you."

"Rory, that can't happen. I won't leave you until I have to, and when I do, then I'll still be in your heart. And if I go and you're still a fine man in your prime, you should find someone else to love."

"No!"

"Yes. I could never go to glory if I thought you'd grieve forever. I'd be a sad wraith, yearning and fading. Do you want that for me?"

"The Lord wouldn't let that happen."

"Then the Lord will find a way for you to carry on and be happy after I'm gone ahead."

"No."

She pushed him away. "Rory. Yes. It will happen, and you will go on with grace so I can rest easy. If you won't agree, then I'll take off this kissing ring, and I'll not see you again."

"You said you'd never put me out!" For the first time in years, she heard the panicked tones of the lonely child he'd been.

She hardened herself against it. If he was to be her man, he must *be* a man, and she must treat him as such.

She retorted, "I said I'd never put the red cat out. He is welcome in my life, always. You, my stubborn darling, are another matter. Now go away and consider prayerfully. Decide which it is to be and then come back and tell me. But don't come back until you decide."

His face went white, but he turned and bolted out of the cottage.

Emer sat down and indulged in a hearty burst of tears.

Before she'd nearly finished, something brushed her ankle.

She sniffed and reached down to lift the red cat into her lap. "Darling Red, you understand, don't you? I love him so, but I can't have him hurting himself like this." She snuffled, and some tears dripped onto the red fur. "This is why wives should be younger than husbands. *We* can survive." Her lips trembled. "When dear old Da passed to glory, Mam was so sad, but when Lambert came for her, she didn't look back. She has Flower now. Flower is worth putting away the sadness."

The red cat got on his haunches and licked tears from her cheeks, peering into her eyes.

He's reading me.

That's all right. I have nothing to hide from my dear red cat.

She closed her arms around him and sobbed.

After a bit, he wriggled free and leapt to the floor, padded across the room and phased through the wall.

Emer wept on.

Rory came back a week before their birthdays.

He tapped on the door for admittance.

Emer opened the door, and they stood staring at one another.

She was shocked at his appearance. He was pale and gaunt, and he'd lost weight to an alarming degree. She supposed she didn't look any better.

He gave her a strained smile, reached out and touched her eyelid. She flinched.

"You've been crying."

"So have you."

"No. Well, only inside." He lifted his chin. "You tried to make new rules."

"I didn't *try*. I just made new rules."

"I have some, too."

"You'd better tell me."

"May I come in?"

"Of course." She gestured to the kitchen. "Sit down."

"I'll do this standing."

She braced herself. She wanted to reach for him, but he looked cool and remote.

"My queen, I will wed you next Wednesday. Master Grene will say the words for us, and we'll be wed before the Lord and witnesses. Mistress Grene and Master and Mistress Pendennis and Master and Mistress Chaucer will stand up with us. We will leave the manse hand-in-hand and come here. We will lie down together and stay there until we want to get up. After that, we will live together in love for as long as we both shall live." He paused and repeated softly, *"For as long as we both shall live.* If one of us goes to glory, the other will live on in love. There will be love for our children and our grandchildren and even beyond. There may be love with another maid or man. That love, if it comes, will be part of a whole. The one who is left of us will be welcome to find a way to love twice over and at the same time." He bit his lip.

"Is that all?"

"It's enough for now. I spent a long time preparing that speech, and I got it all out without interruption and without having to be the red cat. Thank you for listening to me. Is it appropriate?"

She held out her arms. He came into them, and they kissed until her head spun.

"I didn't know you could kiss and cry at the same time," he said.

"I can do many things at the same time." She sobbed a while and said, "What else have you to say, Master Inkersoll?"

"Only this. If I am *ever* such an arse as to make you unhappy again through sheer stubbornness or panic, then you may put me out the door until I'm ready to behave."

Emer hauled him down and kissed him some more until

she was one giant throb of longing.

The kissing rings were failing.

What harm could a week do, really?

You know *what harm. He'll never judge you or anyone else for falling into temptation. He'll only judge himself.*

Chapter Fourteen: Wednesday

December 10, 1952, *The Pixie Forest, Over There*

Emer's wedding to Rory was a quiet affair. Since Emer's father was dead and her mother far away, Mistress Nairn McTavish brought her a traditional gown of braeside wool on the morning of her wedding.

Emer almost wept.

Nairn had two children, but she left them with their father while she came to Emer. She asked, "Did your man like his collar?"

"He says so. He says he'll wear it as long as he lives."

"Right and fitting for a fine priest-to-be." Nairn took Emer's hand. "If you were a young lassie, I'd be bound to give you advice for your bedding night, since your ain mam's not here."

"Maybe you should give it anyway."

"And here's me congratulating myself I'd not need to do that!" Nairn took a deep breath. "Fact is, it's different from how you expect, even if you've been with other laddies. Best thing is to bundle in together and let what will happen, happen. There's only one thing bad to do."

"Oh?"

"If something feels wrong, or hurts over the odds, don't pretend it's not so. If it feels good, *tell him*. That way if you say no to another thing, it's not just *no, no, no*." She puffed out her cheeks. "There, that's said."

"Did *you* say *no* to anything your Cromarty did?" Emer

asked.

"I did not. From what I recall 'twas one hearty *ouch* and a little wait and then a lot of *yes, yes, yes*. It's been *yes, yes, yes* ever since. It's a wonderful thing . . . the stuff of life. But you with your *sight* might know that better than most."

"It's unreliable," Emer said. They shared tea and scones, and then Emer rose to see Nairn out. "What can I give you in exchange for the gown?"

"Och, I was glad to make it. Be happy in it and maybe pass it on to your daughters."

"If I have any."

"You will. You're no' the only lassie with *the sight*." Nairn wrinkled her brow. "Odd, though. It shows me a laddie of my line and Crom's who's somehow bound in marriage with four others."

Emer winced. She'd seen Dornie lose *one* husband. To lose more than one must be intolerable. "Unlucky."

"No. Lucky. At the same time. He's so *happy* in the vision. He's lit up and about to dance. How that will play out I cannot say."

"And how he'll find a priest to say the words?" Emer teased. Then she said, without premeditation. "My Rory would do it, if the love's there. Tell the laddie that."

"Och, he's no' been born and won't be for a long while yet."

Nairn and Cromarty came to see Emer married, so there were eight kind folk wishing them well. Jago Pendennis had made their rings, Berryman Grene said the words, and Catriona, round with her latest child, suggested she should come to the cottage and lie down in their bed.

"It's an old charm for fruitfulness," she said.

"I think we can be fruitful all on our own," Emer said, hugging her.

"Be happy, Emer. I'm still sorry you'll never be my sister,

but you've made your choice, and it's a good choice after all."

"We'll both be happy, Cat. And I hope you'll soon have sisters-by-love to your heart's content."

"Aye, there's a couple of likely lassies casting eyes in that direction."

"It's time for the final blessing," Rory said. He took Emer's hand with a new confidence, and they went to Master Grene's study where they kneeled while he put a hand on each of their heads and commended their happiness into one another's hands.

"What about the red cat?" Emer asked, still kneeling.

"You're not wed to the red cat," Rory said quickly.

"I know, but he's going to be with me as a dear friend for the rest of my life. I'd like some words for him."

"As you wish." Master Grene turned to Rory. "Lad, do as your wife asks. It is a fair and reasonable request."

Rory opened his mouth to protest and then closed it and dropped into his cat-self. Emer scooped him up and hugged him and looked up at Master Grene.

He replaced his hand on her head and laid two fingers on the red cat's head. "And may you two be loving friends from this day forwards as you have been already. Grow in wisdom and affection."

The red cat purred. Emer held him close. "We will."

Master Grene's grandson burst in. "Grandad, Joe's gone home, because you were busy." He looked curiously at Emer, apparently unused to seeing a bride holding a cat. "Oh, you've got the red cat! Are you Mistress Drumwiddy?"

Bemused, Emer shook her head. "Not now, laddie. I'm Mistress Inkersoll."

"He's not waiting anymore then. I'm glad." He lifted his hand as if to stroke the red cat, but Berryman Grene intercepted him and bade him run home because his mother was missing him.

"That's our Peter G, a darling child," he said, watching Emer rise to her feet, still holding the red cat.

A young man tore in, a black-headed pixie with turquoise eyes and a pugnacious jaw. "Greet you, Grandad. Where's Peter G?"

"Gone to Russet, who's looking for him, as usual. What have you done with Pia?"

"Taking tea with Melody and Granny Tess." The young man vanished through the second door.

"*That* is another Peter, and also my grandson, by my daughter, Jestima," Master Grene said to Emer.

"Two Peters?"

"Yes, it's a family name. One is properly Salix Peter. That one just now is Peter Alexis."

"I see. Is he a dear child, too?"

The priest smiled, gazing after the dark-haired young man. "He's a married man, with a little maid, though you mightn't think it. He's wed to a splendid pixie miss named Pia."

"Then why —"

"Why is he looking for my younger grandson? Master Peter Peckerdale has a mind of his own. They're fast friends, young Peter G and that one, despite the years between them. Pia is a strong-minded miss and a loving one. She needs to be both to love the two Peters, though in very different ways."

How odd.

Then Emer chided herself.

And how can you find that friendship odd, with the years between Rory and you? And don't you love Rory and Red?

She recalled that of course she knew of the Peters. Rory had mentioned them, more than once.

The priest turned his attention back to Emer. "Mistress Inkersoll, may I suggest you put your fur friend down? I'm sure Rory wants —"

" . . . a few days free of my studies, Master Grene," Rory said as he landed feet first on the floor.

The priest blinked. "Granted, but as a married man, you should now call me Berry. Peter P does . . . when he's not referring to me as *Grandad* or *that dratted priest.*"

Rory got Emer's hand and agreed yes, he would.

Emer wondered if he'd even heard what the man said.

They left the manse and walked back to the cottage. Emer made tea while Rory prowled about, picking things up and putting them down.

"Stop that," Emer said.

Rory sat in the rocking chair and stared at her with his unblinking amber gaze.

"Stop that." She poured the tea and handed him a cup.

He took a gulp and drew in a pained breath. "Burned my tongue."

"Oh dear, you'll not feel like kissing then." Emer poured too much milk into her cup.

"Give me that." Rory reached for the jug, turned his tea pale and drank it in one long draught. He put the cup down, glanced at Emer and said, "Sorry, my queen. I'm nervous."

Emer swallowed hers likewise. "Master Inkersoll, I think it's time to stop being foolish and get into bed." She barred the door and warded it for good measure, and then walked over to her bed.

No, *their* bed.

She removed her wedding gown and conjured it into her father's old kist. Then she stood in her petticoat. "Rory?"

He came over slowly.

"I'm going to take this off. I know you've seen any number of water maids and tree maids going about their business in their natural state, but I'm not much like them. I'm a lot bigger and a lot softer. Everywhere."

He finally blinked. "I know. I've had my arms around you."

Emer crossed her arms in front of her, caught a double

handful of cloth and hoisted the garment over her head. She untied the ribbon at her waist and let her drawers drop to the floor before conjuring them out of the way. She turned to get into bed.

Rory stopped her. "I'll get in first." He conjured off his clothing, pulled down the counterpane and got between the sheets. He rolled over twice and then rolled back.

"Rory, what are you doing?"

He smiled at her. He was still thin from their estrangement, but his smile was back and bright.

"Mum said my hair was so red it could warm cold sheets. I was warming the bed."

Emer forbore to retort that she'd been standing bare in the cold while he did so. For one thing, it wasn't true. It was early summer. She waited until he turned back the sheet again and then got in beside him.

They lay side by side for a few seconds, and then she rolled in to face him. "Did anyone give you any advice on how to proceed?"

"No. Master Pendennis offered, but then he said it might be better if we muddled it out for ourselves. He's a pisky man, and apparently, *ears* come into it. A lot."

"Let's muddle then." Emer kissed his lower lip and wriggled closer.

He hugged her, pressed his face in her neck and inhaled. He kissed her, arms around her back, and held still. He'd always done that. He said he was afraid of what his hands might do if he let them explore. Emer smoothed her palm down his side to his hip and on down his thigh, touching the sensitive skin with enquiring fingers. He groaned, breathing hard, and after a few seconds, he did the same to her.

"It's . . . I'm—"

She got her mouth on his again and rubbed against him.

His mouth opened in surprise, or possibly in protest. She

wasn't sure which, but she rolled away, pulling him on top of her.

Let's get the ouch over and on to the yes, yes, yes . . .

He said something incomprehensible and pressed sharply into her.

Emer stiffened at the pain and then relaxed into it. It wasn't so bad. She was sure she hadn't made a sound.

He'd noticed, though. He froze. "Emer? What is it?"

She opened her mouth to say it was nothing. Then she said, "It hurt me a wee bit, that's all. If you can hold still like that for a little . . . no, don't pull away. I love being so close to you."

She waited, hearing his rapid breathing. The pain faded. "Now, move again and when you're ready, let go."

He kissed her face gently. "You move. Then you can stop if it hurts."

She chuckled. "Darling Rory, how can I move? I'm pinned down. There's a husband on top of me."

"What if we lie on our sides?"

"We can try." She was seeing the funny side of things. Advice about what to say and how to express appreciation was fine, but how could they manage the practical matters?

Rory rolled off her, bringing her with him so they lay clasped together, facing. Emer was aware of her breasts, unconfined, landing on his shoulder. She choked on another chuckle as he turned his face abruptly to investigate.

"Emer? Are you . . ."

"It's fine." She let the laughter out. "Oh, this is lovely. You can kiss them if you want."

He rubbed his cheek on her. "Maybe after. You're so . . . are you going to move? I feel—"

She moved tentatively against him, pushing her hips and lifting one leg. "Is that—oh—*oh!*" She no longer felt like laughing, moving desperately closer. "Oh!" Her body jerked as a wave of sensation rolled over her.

Rory cried out and moved his face restlessly against her.

The moment passed, and she gave a shaky sigh. "Are you all right?"

"I think I'm meant to ask you that." He swallowed audibly. "Bit of a muddle."

"It was." She let herself sag against him, inhaling his scent. "Rory, do you remember the first time we tried kissing?"

He nodded. "Bit of a muddle then, too. I thought I was going to do something I shouldn't."

"But you didn't. It was fine. So, we need practice, that's all." She ran her fingers down his side again and then touched his face. "We can do all these things now. All the things we didn't put in the kissing rings. Is there anything you've been wanting to do?"

"Well, *that*. Only I expected to be better at it. But I've been wanting to just hold you without any clothes on. And I've longed to sleep with you and to wake up with you."

She let out her breath with a whoosh. "I want that, too."

He tickled her neck. "What were you giggling about?"

"What do you think?"

"Maybe you were happy? You got the giggles when I reminded you I *would* be your man when I had the years for it."

"I think you're right. I'm happy. We muddled through and nobody yelped. I get to have my favourite person in bed with me every night we're not needed elsewhere. I don't have to say goodbye to you at the door."

"Let's not ever say goodbye again."

"We won't, then. If we have to spend a night apart, let's just say *Love you, darling. See you soon.*"

They wriggled about, establishing their preferred way of sleeping, taking turns to put their heads on one another's shoulders and exploring a little. Emer was starting to think a bit more practice would be fun when she realised Rory was asleep. He stretched against her, and she thought of the way the red cat flexed his paws in utter contentment when he slept in her lap.

He's comfortable. He's happy. I love him. I'll have him beside me to love me for the rest of my life.

She kissed his shoulder and drifted into sleep.

In the morning, they practised again, and it was less of a muddle. Emer lay dreamily in her husband's arms and thought back over the last eight years. All that time had led to *this* delightful moment. She was so happy she thought she might never stop smiling.

I'm glad of the sight now. What if I'd been already wed when I met Rory? Any of those braw laddies would have had me at a word. I'd have been good to any of them, and they'd have been good to me. But then I'd meet Rory . . .

She felt a touch of soul-cold at the thought.

We would have been loving friends.

And that, my lassie, would have been a betrayal of your husband and you know it.

Lucky I have the sight, then. It saved me from betrayal.

Rory kissed her shoulder, his red hair bright against her skin. She stroked his cheek, which was a little bristly. She welcomed that. Her darling laddie was now her darling man.

CHAPTER FIFTEEN: FLOWER

1953, The Pixie Forest, Over There

They'd been married for some months when Dornie brought her husband and younger daughter to stay a while in the brae.

They arrived on *Unicorn,* which was a galleon mastered by a hawk-faced galleonfee man. Emer went to meet them and stood hand-in-hand with Rory while they waited for the longboat to bring the family to shore on the pisky coast.

"What will they think of me?" Rory asked.

"They'll love you. Flower will want to meet the red cat right away."

"Does she know how it works?"

"Darling Rory, how could she? I don't know how it works. Even you don't, really." She breathed in the sea air. "More to the point, what will they think of *me*?"

"They'll think we're doing as the good book says, being fruitful and multiplying."

He let go of her hand and put his arms around her, with his palm resting on her stomach. "Have I mentioned how much I love you, my queen?"

"Only every day." She snuggled against him. She knew how happy he was about the coming child. She was happy, too, but she would have liked a little more time with him, just the two of them.

I waited eight years . . .

"Why *queen*, anyway?" She couldn't believe she'd never

asked him that, directly. She'd asked the pisky man, Jago Pendennis, and he'd simply turned the question back on her.

Rory said, "It seems right. I've always thought of you that way. You were so beautiful when I first saw you. I'd never seen anything I wanted so badly as I wanted you."

"When you swung from my skirt as the red kitten?"

"No, when I was lying on the floor with no clothes on. You threw me your shawl and there you were in your petticoat, all big eyes and shining hair and with those big, beautiful . . ." He shifted to fondle the parts in question, his hands decently screened by her shawl

"Rory, you were ten years old. You couldn't possibly have wanted . . ."

"I wanted to sit in your lap and have you cuddle me. That's all. I loved you because you were kind to a heart-sad laddie and you were *you*." He sighed and added in a low voice, "And I knew I was yours and you were mine — forever."

He slipped his hands down to her waist as the longboat grounded with a crunch on the shingle.

Lambert O'Shea made a spry jump and got his feet on land. He helped Dornie out and then held out his arms to his daughter.

Flower let him steady her onto the shore, but her gaze was fixed on Emer and Rory.

"*Go raibh maith agat*, Da."

"That's *thank you*," Emer recalled aloud and half to Rory.

Flower came over to them, and Emer realised how the time had flown. The little dumpling of a sister must be around twelve now. She'd acquired a waist and long reddish curls and the tiny beginnings of breasts. "Emer!"

Emer didn't step away from her husband. No doubt Dervla Flower was used to seeing Lambert cuddle Dornie. Leprechauns were affectionate in word and deed. She wanted to hug her sister in greeting, but she must be a stranger to the child.

I'll let you come to me, pet . . .

She smiled. "Greet you, darlin' Flower. This is my husband, Rory."

Flower fixed sky-blue eyes on Rory. "Red hair? Are you a leppy halfling like me, *deartháir darbh ainm*?"

"Not a halfling, but I have some cousins in the green way, so I'm a little bit leppy. I don't speak the Gaelic, though."

"Oh. Well, I named ye me darlin' brother, since ye're wed to me darlin' sister."

Rory nodded, his chin grazing Emer's hair. "Thank you, sister Flower."

Flower persisted, "And ye're the lad who sent me the oatcake with the carved flower when I was small?"

"And you're the maid who sent me a picture of yourself and your sister."

"That's right. I could do a much better one now." Flower switched her attention to Emer. "You're having a baby."

"Yes. Quite soon."

"Oh *good*. I've got cousins from Da's brother and sister, but they're all older than me. Glory be, I get to be an aunt."

"I'm sure you'll be a good one," Rory said. He seemed entertained, and Emer realised with a pang that he was closer in age to her little sister than to her.

"I will be an excellent aunt. And I'll be a good sister-by-love to ye, Rory. Now . . ." She clasped her hands in supplication. "Please, could I be seeing the red cat?"

Rory rested his cheek on Emer's head. "What do you think, my love? Is this person someone the red cat will find of interest?"

"Of course she is." Emer stepped around so she was embracing him from behind. "Ready?"

They'd practised this.

Rory fixed his attention on the child. "Flower, the red cat won't talk to you, but he'll understand a lot of what you say.

If he rubs his whiskers against you, he's just claiming you into his family. He might stare at you and try to read your soul, but he won't judge whatever he sees. He'll just be wanting to know you. Is that all right?"

Flower nodded, clearly entranced.

Emer kissed Rory's neck and felt him draw in on himself. In a moment, she was holding the red cat around its furry middle. She adjusted him properly into her arms. He purred.

Flower reached out. Emer saw her sister had learned the practical ways of dealing with cats and of course she knew the kelpie, Fash, and her pony companion, Glory-Be.

The transfer was achieved smoothly, and Emer stepped back while Flower stroked the red cat and chatted away in his furry ears.

Emer turned her attention to her mother and father-by-love, who had stood by patiently.

"Mam!" She felt tears in her eyes and held out her arms.

Dornie looked older, but the lines on her face were merry. Lambert looked relaxed and cheerful. If seeing his son-by-love manifest into a cat troubled him, it didn't show.

Emer hugged them both. "Och, it's so lovely to see you both! And Flower's such a fine big—" She paused, glancing at her young sister, who was still engaged with the red cat.

Lassie or colleen?

"We think colleen, darlin'," Lambert said, easily interpreting her hesitation.

"On account of me having some leppy blood and Lambert being a pureblood," Dornie said. Her eyes welled up as she looked at Emer. "You're my lassie, my Emer." She looked down, two tears splashing on her tunic. "Lordie, when is that babe due? You look fit to—"

"A few more weeks," Emer said.

Can't be earlier. Must have got planted on our wedding night as it is.

She added, "How long can you stay?"

"Long enough to see the babby on the move," Dornie said with determination.

Emer smiled. She felt slightly torn about that. She would benefit from Dornie's experience with babies, but Rory was the one she wanted. She longed to see him holding their child.

"We'll be off to the old house at the brae presently," Dornie said.

"Let us know if ye'd like to visit, or if ye'd prefer us to come to ye," Lambert said.

"We'd like to meet your man first though," Dornie put in.

They turned to Flower, still communing with the red cat. The girl lifted a beaming face. "I think Rory wants to come back. Emer, will you take the cat?"

"Set him on the ground," Emer said, and Flower squatted down with an easy grace Emer had to envy.

The red cat put himself to rights, rubbed against Dornie's legs and Lambert's, chirruped at Emer and unfolded into Rory.

Thanks be to the good Lord he can come back with his clothes on!

She said proudly, "Rory, here are Mam and Lambert. Mam, this is my Rory."

Dornie held out her hand, but Rory, after a glance at Emer, put both hands on her shoulders and kissed her brow. "Mistress O'Shea, it's lovely to meet you." He turned to the leprechaun man, who grinned at him and held out his arms.

Rory went into them without hesitation, and the men hugged.

"Thanks be to Patrick and Mary, ye're the very man for our Emer. You and I are the luckiest o' men . . . an' when our Dervla Flower makes *her* choice, there'll be one more o' us," Lambert said, stepping back.

"And I hear *you* rode all the way here on a kelpie to secure your bride. A *kelpie,* man!"

"So I did. I meant to take my Dornie home and wed her in fine style at Erin a' Fee, but when it came to the push, I couldn't wait to be hers in ivery way . . . if ye take me meaning. We stopped off at the pisky coast and had the Master o' *Unicorn* row out an' say the words over us. Had to stand in the water, for the spalpeen would niver set his foot on land."

Emer felt her eyebrows rise. She'd never known where and when that wedding had taken place. "What about Fash?"

The leprechaun laughed. "Fash was our witness, belly-deep, along wid the master's lady sitting her side-saddle." He looked speculatively at Rory. "Seems to me ye could give us a do-over on dry land."

"I'm not a parson yet."

"Ye will be."

"Another two and a bit years 'til the bishop will see him," Emer said.

"Then we'll be here at that time, and ye'll say the words over us again."

"My hand on it," Rory said.

Emer's back was aching, so she suggested they should head for home.

Dornie wanted to go to the brae house, but before they set off, Lambert drew Emer aside.

"I know I took away your mam an' left ye alone."

"Och, I was happy for her, I promise you. I've managed well, and now I have Rory. It's grand to see you all again, but everything is for the best."

"Sure, I believe that." He added softly, "Have ye needed the kelpie bottle wish yet?"

"No . . . I haven't forgotten it. I have it safe in Da's old kist, but I've needed nothing." She reflected on the horrible, but fortunately brief, period of her estrangement from Rory. Why had she not used the kelpie bottle then?

Och, the decision had to be his. If I'd used a wish, I'd never have known if his mind was truly accepting or if he'd been nudged into it.

"Lambert, it was so kind of you to give it to me, and it has been a comfort, but would you like it back, for Flower, maybe?"

"No, darlin' Emer. That's a mite of help for ye . . . just in case. Once it's used, hand it on to someone else. But ye're right not to use it on a whim. Best kept for something important."

Dornie called him, and she and her man went off to the brae, while Flower accompanied her sister and Rory to the cottage.

The child chattered to both of them, and Emer began to see flashes of the little maid she remembered. When they arrived at the cottage by the pixie forest, Flower asked, "Would you like me to rub your back, Emer? I have the *loving touch*, but in me, it works wid the body, not the soul."

Emer didn't hesitate. "That would be wonderful, Flower. Rory will make us tea and get oatcakes. Do you remember his oatcakes?"

"I do that!" Flower looked about. "I love your crystals. Look." She felt in her pouch and extracted the wooden flower with the crystal in the centre. "This is my favourite thing. When I make my gossoon mine, I want him to be as lovin' as your Rory is to you."

"That will be a wee while yet," Emer said.

"Sure, I have me eye on him already," Flower said cheerfully. She grinned. "Red hair, he has, fit to warm the bed when we get one, and skin the shade o' fresh barley straw." She kissed her fingers.

Emer bit her lip as she heard a tiny gasp of laughter from her husband. Surely Flower was making a joke? But then she remembered Rory's words . . ."*I knew I was yours and you were mine . . .*" He'd been ten.

Lucky I didn't know then. I'd have had *to send him away. For once, deluding myself was a good thing . . .*

CHAPTER SIXTEEN: SISTER OF MY HEART

1953, *The Pixie Forest, Over There*

"First, a hug though," Flower said and put her arms around Emer. She stretched up to kiss her cheek. "I've missed ye, *deirfiúr mo chroí*," she whispered.

"I've missed you, too, dearie," Emer responded. She heard her voice wobble and made no attempt at the Gaelic endearment, though she knew it meant *sister of my heart*. A tear ran down her cheek as she realised how much of Flower's young life she'd missed. To distract her doleful thoughts, she breathed in the wholesome scent of clover blossoms that characterised Flower's skin and hair.

Flower must have been inhaling memories, too, for she said cheerfully, "Ye'll have to teach me the way of making oatcakes, *acushla*. Now, lie ye down."

Emer moved over to the bed and lay as flat on the bed as the baby-bulk would allow. She conjured off her gown and petticoat.

"Rory, keep your eyes on your work," Flower said severely.

Rory's laughter bubbled up audibly. "Flower, don't you think I've seen my sweet wife bare and beautiful before?"

"I should hope ye have! But I'd not want ye sloppin' the tay or droolin' in it."

Flower took a small pot of balm from her pouch and kneeled on the bed beside Emer. She scooped out a dollop and rubbed her palms together, and then she put her small, capable hands on Emer's back.

Warmth spread from them, and the ache subsided.

Emer sighed. The relief was so great she soon went to sleep.

She woke to see Flower drinking tea and chatting with Rory. He was responding equably, but his amber gaze was on Emer. As soon as she stirred, he came to her and helped her to sit up, wrapped her in a shawl and handed her a cup.

"Good nap, my queen?"

"Yes. I feel fine." She really did.

Flower drained her cup. "Mam told me the way to take to the brae house. I'll be off now and leave ye two together. Rory, keep Emer warm and see if she'll take a little gentle exercise. I believe it's a good way for promotin' restful sleep." She came over and kissed them both, promised to return for her oat-cake-making lesson, and then let herself out of the cottage.

Emer met Rory's dancing gaze. "Do you think . . ."

"I do think. That sister of yours is a maid with far too much knowledge for her age. She told me you'd feel well enough for what she termed *enough years matters*."

"What did you say to that?"

"I said *thank you, deirfiúr le grá*, and I hoped I got it right." He watched as Emer drank her tea. "Did I? Do you?"

"You did. And what do you think?" She unwrapped the shawl and got into bed.

Rory stripped and dived in after her. "My queen."

"Always," she said as she opened herself to pleasure.

Chapter Seventeen: Davey and Andorie

September 1953, *The Pixie Forest, Over There*

Emer woke with a backache.

She groaned. "Rory, would you send for Flower? My back—"

A low pain sent her out of bed and off to the privy.

It's too early . . .

She steadied herself. Dornie had said the baby would come sooner than Emer thought. Emer's *sight* kept giving her confusing images. She was sure she was giving Rory a son, but Nairn McTavish insisted she carried a daughter.

I just hope it's not a litter.

She caught herself up sharply. There would be no kittens until the child was ten or so, and probably not then. The manifestation Rory and Master Pendennis carried was rare and never developed in babies.

She emerged from the privy to find Rory scribbling a note.

She put her hand on his. "Not Flower."

"But you said you wanted her."

"It's not what I thought. It's your son. He's on his way to the world."

She thought Rory would be alarmed, but he set the paper down and gave her a brilliant smile.

"Tell me what you'd like."

"A tub?" she said hopefully.

"A tub it will be. I'll make you tea, and then I'll come in with you."

"In the tub?"

"No, in the bed. Mistress McTavish gave me a blanket to put on the bed, and Mistress Grene explained what I should do. Or maybe you'd rather have your mum?"

"I want you."

He warmed a tub and helped Emer into it. The pains came and faded. They were growing in severity.

Emer tried to focus on her son-to-be.

Rory brought her tea and then helped her to their bed, which he covered with a blanket woven of the softest braeside wool. He took off his clothing and lay beside her, gathering her into his arms.

"I'm going to kiss you as much as you want, *if* you want, and don't worry about biting me or saying *not now*."

He sounded so certain. Emer gave a sob of thankfulness.

The day wore along, and Emer found she could sleep between pains until close to the end when a new sensation almost overwhelmed her.

"You know how your body takes over when we're loving one another? Let it take over now," Rory said. He held her warmly, and she spaced out, letting things happen.

"Here he comes." Rory kissed her belly and took his son gently by the shoulders. "Greet you, and welcome to the world, sweet Davey!"

Emer flopped, exhausted. Then she said, "Davey?"

"I've been thinking of him that way, but we can name him whatever you wish." Rory wrapped his son in a soft blanket, kissed him, and then he handed him to Emer.

"Davey is fine. My old da was called David," she said. She felt lightheaded and unreal. Their baby was perfect. So was the name.

"Lie down with us?" she asked Rory.

He looked at her lovingly and then frowned. He put his hand on her stomach.

"It'll go flat again . . . well, as flat as I ever am. Just a wee bit stretched — " She broke off with an indignant gasp as a new pain surged over her.

"That will be the . . ." Rory had apparently forgotten the word, but he made himself ready anyway.

The look on his face a few minutes later would have sent Emer off into giggles if she'd been in any state to laugh.

"Holy Mary!" Rory exclaimed as a second baby arrived with a rush and landed in his hands.

"Better welcome her, too," Emer said, panting.

"Her?"

"Nairn said there would be a lassie. I owe her a wee apology."

Rory hugged the baby, who spluttered and opened light-coloured eyes. "Greet you, my little lassie. We'll think of a sweet name for you."

"Andorie, after your mam and mine," Emer said. The name had been in the back of her mind but she'd not expected to use it for a while yet.

"Perfect."

"I think you have to cut the cords."

"Oh. Yes." He gave her their daughter and dealt with the rest of the process. He lovingly sponged Emer and the babies and then conjured a fresh blanket. He said a heartfelt prayer of thanks. Then he got on the bed with Emer. "My darling queen, I think we're going to be busy."

They were.

Chapter Eighteen: Mathias Charming

December 1955, *The Pixie Forest, Over There*

Soon after Rory's twenty-first birthday and Emer's thirty-third, Rory was sitting on the floor with a set of bagpipes in his lap, making them squawk and wail to amuse the twins.

"What kind of row is that?" Emer asked.

"Caterwauling, my queen, as befits the main man of the red cat."

She bent and kissed him, laughing.

The tap on the door barely registered in her mind until Andorie looked up. She had amber eyes like Rory and very quick hearing.

"Door?"

"That's Flower, I suppose . . . come in, hen!" Emer conjured the door open and turned to greet her sister.

She was taken aback when Master Berryman Grene stepped over the threshold.

He'd been there before, first to baptise the twins, and several times since to work with Rory. As he explained, it was easier for him to come to them than for Rory to leave Emer and the children.

She was grateful to the kind old man for that. She'd sometimes thought a bit coldly of Master Grene when Rory was young, but she saw now that the man had done the best he could for his orphaned charge.

And who am I to think hardly of anyone? I left him alone for close to two years.

He'd never once chided her about that. In fact, he said it was a good thing. It allowed him to pass from child to young man and meet her again on a more even footing. He'd never said much about the way he'd spent that time, and she'd never wanted to ask. She also never enquired about how the Grenes felt when their charge, still young, had taken to spending what must have been a lot of time alone in a cottage, waiting for its mistress to come back.

What surprised her was that Master Grene had brought a stranger with him—a fine-looking personage with a broad face, thick brown hair and bright blue eyes.

"Greet you, Berryman, and you, master," Emer said.

"Emer, this is His Grace, Bishop Mathias Charming," Master Grene said. "Matt, this is Mistress Emer Inkersoll, and these two scamps are Davey and Andorie."

The bishop held out his hand, and Emer glanced at Rory.

Do I shake it or kiss it? Should I curtsy?

The bishop said softly, "Greet you, Mistress Inkersoll." He took her hand in a warm clasp and looked her over.

Emer wished she'd had time to put on something better than her garden gown. She could conjure something, but that might look odd.

She smiled to hide her chagrin. "Would you like tea, Master Charming?"

"That would be grand if you have t' time."

Hob.

"You're not wearing a smock," she said without intending to.

The bishop laughed. "I do at home *over here,* mistress. Fortunately for my comfort, the vestments I wear on official duty *over there* are fulsome enough for me to feel decently clad."

Master Grene said, "The man with the pipes is Rory Inkersoll, and this lassie's husband, as you may have gathered."

Rory untangled himself from Davey and the bagpipes. "Greet you, Your Grace. Have you come to examine me on doctrine?" His voice sounded apprehensive, and Emer realised anew how much his calling meant to him. He'd been so busy as her husband and the twins' father he'd probably not studied as much as he should. She felt sorry about that, but she trusted the Lord knew how much she needed him.

The bishop turned to study him as he had Emer. "Greet you, Master Inkersoll."

"Rory."

"I can see why." He glanced at the twins. "You've stamped those two wi' t' blood."

Emer had to agree he had. Andorie had her father's amber eyes, and Davey's hair was an emphatic red. She moved to make the tea. The kettle was hot already.

"Do you think I should?" the bishop said.

Should? What? Oh, examine him on doctrine . . .

Rory said, "I'm not the greatest scholar."

"Indeed?"

"We keep him too busy, Master Charming," Emer said.

Davey patted Rory's knee. Rory swung his son up and kissed him.

Emer poured the tea and set out oatcakes and some preserves with bread and cheese. She had no idea what bishops ate, but she knew hobs had hearty appetites. This one was difficult to read, with the hob dialect coming and going in his voice. She wondered what the red cat would make of him. The red cat had a great deal of wisdom.

She indicated the spread, and then she removed Andorie before she got her fingers into the quince jelly.

The men sat at the table and Rory took Andorie while Emer drank her tea. He passed her back and took up his own, pausing to cut a piece of cheese for Davey, who loved it.

"Would you like me to go out with the twins while you talk?" Emer asked presently.

The bishop gave her a quick smile. "Not at all, Mistress. This is your home. If anyone should go out, it's me. As for talking, I've seen all I need of Master Rory here. If you'd all care to come to St Botolph's . . . thank you, lad. Tha's right kind of thee." He took the piece of bread Davey offered and put it into his mouth.

"You have bairns," Emer said.

"Indeed, I do. How did you know?"

"Emer has *the sight*," Master Grene said.

"A lot of braeside lassies do."

"It wasn't that, but folk without bairns don't normally look so comfortable with them," Emer said.

"My forever and I have three delightful maids . . . Nancy, Pauline and Carol. I hope you'll meet them when . . . where was I?"

"You mentioned St Botolph's," Rory said.

"Aye well, 'tis t' church where I'd prefer to ordain you. We could do it here, but the gateway church is more fitting, since tha'll have t' ordering of it when Berryman steps back." He took another oatcake.

Rory went pale under his thatch of red hair. "But don't you need to question me on things?"

"I could if you insist, but I'd rather have another cup of tea. Do you permit, Mistress Emer?"

"Of course."

Emer watched as the bishop conjured the teapot and poured himself more tea. He took a third oatcake.

"Thank you, lad. A perfect accompaniment." He accepted some cheese from Davey and ate that, too.

Davey's in favour of him, anyway. He generally gives cheese only to Andorie.

Emer smiled over the thought. Her Davey loved food and music and seeking beetles in the garden. He had decided opinions, and she loved him dearly. He wasn't much like her, or, indeed, like Rory. He was what her old da used to call *his ain self.*

Maybe he's like Da?

She'd tried to see her beloved father when he was young, but that was something *the sight* had never cared to show her.

Now that she came to think of it, she realised *the sight* had been all but absent since the twins' birth.

Too busy in the here and now to be peering into the then and the maybe . . .

When their guests had gone, Rory sat down with a plop in Emer's rocking chair, knocking the quilted cushion askew. His hands were shaking.

Emer was about to take them when she heard another tap on the door.

I hope that's not another bishop. That one was kindly, but poor Rory couldn't face up to two.

Flower popped her head in. "Greet ye, darlin's . . . may I have my nievies?"

"Please do," Emer said.

The twins were already in motion, scurrying over to grab Flower by the hands. They went out, bouncing and delighted.

Silence reigned. Emer looked at Rory. He was still shaking with reaction.

"What's wrong, my love?"

He favoured her with his unblinking gaze and folded suddenly into the red cat.

Emer picked him up and carried him into their bedroom. Since the twins' birth, they'd moved into another room to offer a modicum of privacy. Her old tub rule carried forth to the bedroom rule for the twins. The tub was open to all of them. The bed was for her and Rory. She sat on the bed and swung her feet up, settling the red cat beside her. She tickled his ears, enjoying the quiet and feeling him slowly relax.

When he'd been purring for a while, she said, "Rory?"

Her husband unfolded.

"You forgot your clothes."

"I didn't."

Emer conjured off her gown, and they got into bed.

"That was a muddle," he said.

She kissed his shoulder. "It wasn't. It was exactly right. Asking you questions wouldn't tell that hob man who you are. Watching you being you is what he wanted."

"Is being me enough?"

"Being you will always be enough, my love. Husband, father, and now you're to be a father to others. In the manner of speaking. You will be extraordinary, as always." She rolled in and opened her arms. "Rory, do you want more bairns?"

"Maybe someday. Not yet. I'll be away more soon."

"I have ten or maybe twelve more years before I'm too old."

He stroked her breast. "My own queen, you will never be too old."

"Not for *this*," she agreed, chuckling as he entered her with an energetic thrust. "Ooh, that's lovely." She put back her head to watch his eyes, dilated with passion for her. "But too old for bearing bairns."

"Maybe we could wait three or four years?" He pressed in hard, moving his hips to maximise her pleasure.

Emer felt her tension mounting and panted, putting it off. "Three years is — oh, Rory, *yes, yes, yes!*" There was no delaying it after all.

She watched his eyes darken and drew him close to her breast.

He moaned, shuddered, and kissed her. "My queen, I'm so happy I could — ooh!"

"Ooh?" Emer suddenly felt what he meant. "*Ooh! We're going again!*"

Flower brought the twins back, tired and happy after playing in a pool with the waterfolk children. Waterfolk swam from babyhood, and Davey and Andorie were surprisingly at home in the water.

Rory swam well, too, and his capacity for spending time underwater without needing to breathe offered probable proof of the sylvan ancestry he'd mentioned.

Emer was occasionally troubled by the notion he might stop visibly ageing before he was thirty, as full sylvan did, but she put the idea away.

What will happen, will happen, and he can't be very much sylvan, or he'd have a maid morph.

She was sure he hadn't. The red cat was male and must be Rory's only other form.

Flower stayed to supper. After the twins were in bed, she said abruptly, "I'm going to miss you all *so* much when we go back to Erin a' Fee."

"When's that, then?" Emer had hoped Dornie and her man might have decided to stay in the brae.

"Soon, though I'll be back this way in a year or so for sponsorin'. Mam said ye'd take me to darlin' Kerry."

Emer said she would, though she wondered how it would be, going back *over there* after so long.

And how do we get to Kerry's? Since my time with her, she's always come here!

"Fine, Mam an' Da were waiting until ye could say the words over them," Flower went on. "Da's got a fancy for a weddin' on the dry earth. Now Rory's going to be priested that can happen."

"How did you know?" Rory asked.

Flower gave him a reproving look. "Sure, what else were ye doin' wid that bishop?"

"Feeding him," Emer said and laughed.

CHAPTER NINETEEN: HAZEL

January 1956, *St Botolph's Gateway Church*

Early in the new year, Rory and Emer went through the St Botolph's gateway to *over there*. The church and its environs were warded, so it was a comfortable place.

Before they left for the gateway, Emer expected Rory to be jittering with nerves, but her husband surprised her with his calm.

She watched his dear face as he made breakfast for the twins and recalled his gentle certainty on the day of their birth.

He was dressed as usual in his britches and tunic, but what followed was a little less than usual. Master Grene called for them with a horse and cart, and to Emer's surprise, Rory took the reins. She supposed she should have known he could drive. The horse, a fay mare named Dorcas, stamped her forehooves in turn, apparently eager for the journey.

"She knows there's a feed of clover hay waiting for her at the gateway stables," Mistress Grene said, catching Emer's eye as she settled Andorie beside her on the padded seat.

A green ring glowed on her finger, and Emer, as usual, wondered at its beauty. One day, she might ask its pedigree, but maybe not now.

She tucked her arm around Davey, who wanted to join his father on the driving seat.

"No, my laddie, here with me," she said.

Master and Mistress Grene and their grandson, the

younger Peter, shared the seating.

"If everybody is ready?" Rory asked.

They called the affirmative, and Rory relaxed his grip on the reins. Dorcas tossed her head and set forth at a determined trot.

Their way led through the brae, where they paused to fetch Dornie, Lambert and Flower.

"We'll perch at the back," Dornie said cheerfully, as Emer hoisted Davey onto her lap to make room.

"I can do that, Mam. You sit here with Mistress Grene," Emer said.

"Peter G—" Mistress Grene began.

Dornie laughed. "No need. I'm no' so old I can't dangle me feet in the breezes. Besides, it will take me back to my wedding journey riding double with Lambert on Fash."

"Fash?" Mistress Grene looked bemused.

"Fash is a kelpie mare from Erin a' Fee," Emer explained with a chuckle. She recalled her own journey and wondered, not for the first time, what Fash and her pony companion, Glory-Be, made of their O'Shea family's long absence. There was good grazing at Erin a' Fee, and no doubt Cormac and Dervla had been charged with providing such treats and friendly attention as the equine companions might want.

It occurred to her to wonder just why Fash had stayed on at the house in Rósanna Locha after she'd done her wish duty. According to Lambert, the kelpie bottle had *brought* her to carry him, implying she must have come from elsewhere. Well, she must have found the place, or possibly Glory-Be's companionship, to her taste.

While she mused, Rory got Dorcas underway again, and the next thing Emer knew they were drawing up at the St Botolph's gateway.

Rory brought Dorcas to a proper halt and bounded down from the driving seat. He conjured an armful of clover hay from the airy wooden building everyone called *the gateway stables*. He unharnessed the mare, who snorted, gave him a friendly nudge, and took a mouthful of the fragrant hay.

Rory patted her and then helped Emer and the twins down from the cart.

Emer needed no help, but she knew Rory loved to give it.

They turned to the gateway, where they all took hands as was usual when stepping between realms.

Lambert looked uncertain, and Emer realised that, as a green gossoon, he would never have spent time *over there*.

Master Grene assured them the folk at St Botolph's would have better manners than to stare.

"Most of them are at least trace fay anyway. The full humans among them attend in the full knowledge of what style of church it is."

Lambert nodded. "They might stare at our ladies, though, as fine as they are," he remarked.

Emer agreed that they were very fine. Dornie had on a traditional colleen's festival dress, which shouldn't have suited her taller figure, but which looked just right. The bright green and clover-pink layers were startling, but Lambert couldn't have looked prouder of his pretty wife. Emer wore her Drumwiddy plaid wedding dress, feeling it was the only thing fine enough for the occasion. Dornie had made her a lace collar to ornament it, and her crystal necklace glittered against the white folds.

Mistress Grene was resplendent in a summer gown of lavender and pixie green, while Flower had a smaller version of Dornie's dress. Andorie was too young to care much with what she wore, but Emer had sewn her a tunic in amber linen which matched her eyes. Davey had the shorter lad's version in fox-red.

She heard Lambert take an audible breath before Dornie and Flower drew him over the threshold in the wake of the others and across the short walk to the churchyard.

The church was built from local stone, but it had a timeless quality and a feeling of peace. Emer was glad Rory would be *priested,* as Flower put it, in such lovely surroundings. She looked around in a vaguely proprietary manner. This was where her Rory would preach, and sing, and nurture his flock for years to come.

Bishop Charming awaited them at the door to the church. He greeted everyone and then sent them inside while he and Rory went to the vestry with Master Grene.

Emer joined in with the first hymn, glad Flower and young Peter G were there to help contain the twins.

Master Grene conducted the service until the point where Rory came to be introduced to the congregation.

Emer caught her breath as her husband stepped out of the vestry. He wore a long black garment she remembered was a cassock and the collar she had made for him. He had added a string of three crystals which caught the light from the candles.

Emer's heart swelled with love and pride.

My man, my Rory, och, look at him now! What a pity Red can't be here to see . . .

She caught herself up at that with a tiny gasp that was not quite a giggle.

Her next thought removed any temptation to laughter.

His mother is missing this . . . and what of his father? They should be here to share the joy. So should Da —

She broke that thought off in a hurry. If David Drumwiddy had been here to see his son-by-love taking up his calling, then Lambert would not be hugging his wife to him with a proprietary arm.

And Flower would never have been born.

Emer resolved to be happy with those who were with her today. She wouldn't wish for those who were gone.

She had little idea of what to expect of what Flower termed

Rory's priesting, but the ceremony was surprisingly short and simple.

As Mathias Charming explained, an ordination into the St Botolph's church was rather like a wedding. Rory was entering into a new family while maintaining his accustomed place in his own. He would act as a curate for the first year, after which Master Grene would step back to leave him in charge.

The questions and answers did sound like a wedding, and after it was over, Emer was warmed to see members of the congregation, friends and strangers, welcoming her husband into their hearts. She'd expected to efface herself, but at the reception, which was held at the church hall, Rory picked up Andorie and held out his hand for Emer to join him.

Emer looked about for Davey and found him sitting on a stool and conversing with the bishop, whom he had evidently liked and remembered.

She relaxed, talking, smiling, listening and inwardly raising her brows at the odd clothing the more human congregationers wore. She was glad she'd put on her fine wedding dress of Drumwiddy plaid. It was a little loose, as the twins kept her on the move, but Rory's eyes had assured her she was still the most beautiful lassie he'd ever seen.

After the first half-hour, the bishop's wife drew Emer aside.

Mistress Charming, to Emer's astonishment, was fully human. Her name was Hazel, and she had a plump and smiling face, curly brown hair and warm eyes. She professed herself more than happy to welcome *another church-wife,* as she put it.

"I think married priests give folk confidence, especially if they have kiddies. Matt and I had our three close together so they'd be company for one another, but you did even better, having twins. Are you planning any more, Missus Inkersoll?"

"Emer. And we're hoping so, in three years or so," Emer said. She gazed at Hazel Charming, who wore a blue-flowered gown with a lot of cloth in it, held in with a buckled belt covered in the same cloth. Surely the fashions were mostly skimpier *over here*? The other human ladies in the congregation were mostly bare-shouldered, although they wore becoming hats. Even the pisky miss and her young daughter over talking to Flower wore minimal silver for their order — unless they had covered the bulk of it with a glamour.

Are they from Master Jago's family?

The set of the eyes looked familiar from both the pisky jeweller and his mani-self, Master Floppy.

Her attention came back to the wide blue floral skirts that swung around Hazel's neat calves.

That must be more than a full circle skirt.

The other woman caught her interest and smiled. "I wear belts in public to confine all the gathers, Missus Inkersoll — Emer. You know how hobs are."

"I know they eat a lot," Emer said cautiously.

"They wear a lot, too, and they love lots of cloth on their wives! I can dress to please myself, naturally, but I choose to please Matt, though I draw the line at smocks. I had enough of those while I was expecting. We all want to be beautiful in the eyes of our husband, I think, so if he loves big frocks, then I'm happy to wear them for him." Her smile broadened. "You certainly are beautiful. Your husband's pride in you is palpable. But no — pride is the wrong word, I think. It's more as if he can't believe his good fortune at having won such an Earthly treasure. Have you been married long?"

"Just over three years. The twins came a wee bit early, but I think we must have planted them on our first bedding."

Hazel's lips twitched.

"Och, have I said something wrong?"

"Not at all. It's just that most folk I know don't speak much of *bedding* unless they're talking about plants. Matt does, of course, though he keeps it between our rectory walls. Hobs have a fine appetite for what my husband is pleased to call *all the fine things t' good Lord has seen fit to offer us.* For all that, he's kind and gentle, and when we got married, he gave me the choice about . . . er . . . nightwear. My nighties are formidable affairs with more cloth than is typically found in a wedding gown!" She added reflectively, "I can tell you that Matt and his ways made a refreshing change from some of the boys I knew before . . ." She caught herself up. "This is rather inappropriate talk for a church environs. Maybe we can get together sometime and gossip about our husbands and kiddies. Do you come *over here* often?"

"This is the first time in eighteen-odd years," Emer said.

"Really?"

"Aye, when I go to divine service, it's been at the manse, and that no' as often as maybe I should. Mind, I'll need to be back and forth a wee bit when my sister comes over in a year or so." She explained about Flower and Dornie's cousin, Kerry, who would sponsor her.

"Would that be Kerry Palmer by any chance? I know she sometimes has young folk staying from *over there*. She runs a holiday house she calls *Fayhaven*, but I do believe that's mostly a front for its real purpose."

"Aye, that's her name. She took me in at *Fayhaven* back then when it was my turn to try learning to *pass*."

"I do know her, then! She's a grand hand with baking, and we've drunk a lot of tea and eaten far too many scones together. When I first met her, I thought she was Irish, but Matt explained she's a leprechaun colleen. She's a nice woman and very warm and friendly. I don't need to tell you that, though."

Emer nodded. "She comes to visit us once in a wee while. She's been a time or two since Mam's been back in the brae."

After that, naturally, she had to explain about Dornie's marriage with Lambert and how she came to have a sister so much younger . . . and a colleen at that. As she spoke, answering and asking questions, she felt both comfortably at home and extraordinarily out of place.

Chapter Twenty: Little John

January 1956, *St Botolph's Gateway Church Hall*

Emer was about to say she really should see to the twins when a hob maid wearing a pink tent dress beckoned them over to a serving hatch where morning tea was offered to a line-up of parishioners with cups.

"Matt's niece, Annya," Hazel murmured. She urged Emer into the line, and soon Emer reached the hatch, where she was served by a tall young man with red hair and freckles. He had a long face and a stubborn chin, but his eyes, almond-shaped and hazel-green, were friendly. He tilted a flowered teapot towards Emer's cup and raised his brows. "Tea, ma'am, or would you prefer coffee?" He had a deep and pleasant voice.

"Tea please, master, with a wee bit of milk." She couldn't help staring at his bright hair. It was every bit as red as Rory's.

He poured, neatly and quickly, and indicated a jug of milk and a bowl of white lumps Emer remembered as sugar. "Help yourself to milk and sugar, ma'am."

Ma'am? Perhaps her disconcerted feeling at the honorific showed in her eyes, because he smiled.

"I beg your pardon — you must be one of the fairy ladies . . . fay, right?"

"Fairy or fay, makes no odds," Emer said.

"So I should have said *mistress*, not ma'am —"

"Call me Emer, laddie. I'm just a wee bit flummoxed by all the folk here."

He laughed then, his eyes crinkling. "And not only by *folk,*

I think! You sound just like my mum, mistress . . . Emer." He nodded towards an armchair, where an ancient woman sat determinedly upright, balancing a cup and saucer in one hand and a small plate of strawberries in the other. In defiance of the summery weather, she wore a black wool gown with a heather-coloured shawl. The young man said, "Mum's a Scot from Argyllshire, and she always calls me laddie."

"You're no' Scottish, though?" Emer asked.

"I was born in New South Wales. Mum came out here with her husband when she was twenty . . . Go and say hello to her, if you want. Her hearing's still pretty good, and she sings hymns with the best of them."

Emer said, "I didn't see you in church."

"I crept in at the back with Mum during the first hymn. If I'd been up front, you'd hardly have missed me, would you?"

He indicated his hair. His eyes danced with fun, and she knew he knew she'd been staring.

"I beg your pardon . . . but I don't often see folk with hair that colour outside of our family. It's as bright as my husband's and my wee son's."

"You're married to the new parson, then, mistress, and it will be your little boy discussing cheese with the bishop? They came by for tea . . . or milk, in your boy's case . . . a few minutes back, and I'm sure I heard the terms cheddar and double Gloucester . . . oh, and something about fay goats' cheese? Do I have that right?"

A woman standing next to Emer cleared her throat and gestured to the teapot the young man still held. "*If* you please, young man, some of the rest of us would also like some tea."

The young man mouthed *whoops!* to Emer and turned his attention to the woman who'd spoken.

"Sorry, Missus Raintree. I have tea or coffee, and you help yourself to milk and sugar. What will it be?"

"Tea, I said, if you'd been listening," the woman said in an exasperated voice.

Emer moved along hastily and came up with Hazel Charming, who had been served by the pink-clad Annya, and who was waiting for her.

"I see little John was practising his charms on you," Hazel said lightly.

"*Little* John? He's taller than most!"

"Figure of speech, from an old tale," Hazel said.

Ah, Robin Hood! It was one of the stories common to fay and human.

"He thought I sounded Scottish, like his mam," Emer said, in explanation.

"Elsie Folly is determinedly Scottish, though she's lived here in Australia for many years. Shall I introduce you? She's quite a character. I know *you're* not a Scot, but you do sound like one to the untutored ear, so you'll have no problems tuning in to her accent. She's a formidable woman, and she doesn't suffer fools. She calls a spade a spade, as my dad would say. I like her."

Emer looked over at the upright old lady, who was now conversing with Clover Grene. Her dark clothing formed a sombre contrast to Mistress Grene's pixie gown.

"Maybe next time," she said. She cleared her throat. "She's a wee bit old to be that laddie's mother."

Hazel ushered her over to a small table, where they sat down and observed the mingling congregation. "Elsie's age is one of the mysteries into which I choose not to enquire. I suspect she's Little John's grandmother, or even further removed than that. He can't be more than twenty-seven or so, can he?"

"Around that, I'd say," Emer agreed.

Hazel mused, "Perhaps she adopted him from some other family member. It's not my business to know her private affairs, and I shudder to think what she'd say if she thought I was prying.

"Oh, don't look like that, Emer. I know *you* weren't prying, and it's a natural thing to wonder. Whatever the blood relationship between those two, I'm sure there is one. Just look at the curve of the brow . . . and they both have a slightly crooked little finger . . . although in Elsie's case, it might be arthritis. Her hair must have been red when she was younger. You can tell it's got gold shades in it even now. Red hair's a recessive gene."

"He's a good deal taller than her, I should think," Emer said. The old lady was seated, but straight-backed though she was, Clover Grene towered over her, and Clover was not abnormally tall, for a pixie.

"Maybe his father or his real mother was tall."

Emer sipped her tea and glanced back at the red-headed young man, who was filling cups for the pisky woman and her daughter, who were surely Pendennises by blood, if not by name. Something about the line of his profile caught at her attention with a feeling of déjà vu, but after a moment she shook her head, telling herself not to be fanciful. She was sure she'd never met him before. She'd have remembered that hair, and besides, he was human.

She looked around for Rory and spotted him half-submerged in a crowd of parishioners. Andorie was on his shoulders.

I'll stay here. He'll be able to see me and come over when he has time.

They drank their tea and ate scones and some excellent cake, which Hazel produced from her bag in a greaseproof paper wrapping.

"My Matt made this," Hazel said, as Emer bit into a fragrant slice. "I can cook, of course, but I defy any human to touch a hob man for baking. This is hob courting cake, and you and I shall eat it in friendship." She smiled and added, gently, "You know, of course, that it's charmed, but *it will do no harm to thee or me*, as Matt likes to put it. He and I shared a courting cake on our wedding night, and he explained to me then that it is meant to be shared between *true souls*. That's why I had it in my bag, rather than putting it out on the tables."

Emer, who had hesitated after that first bite, relaxed. The charm was a gentle and kindly one, as hob charms always were. When she'd finished the cake, which was as good as Hazel claimed, she said, "My Rory is a fine baker. He makes oatcake to my mam's recipe. I taught him how when he was a bairn, and now, he bakes better than I do."

It occurred to her to wonder where Dornie was, but she assumed her mother would be with Lambert, who must, as the only green gossoon in the congregation, feel even more out of place than she did.

She glanced again at Rory and then back at the young man called John. The noise of conversation and the clink of crockery washed over her, and she suddenly longed to be back at the cottage with Rory and the twins where she knew what was what, and where there were no disconcerting images and half-seen memories.

Chapter Twenty-one: The Court-ship of Matt and Hazel

January 1956, *St Botolph's Gateway Church Hall and Garden*

Hazel must have noticed her unease, for she set down her cup and said, "Maybe we could go for a walk around the church and look at the gardens. Your husband is going to be busy for a while. Father Grene is well-loved, but a new young priest is a novelty, especially one as handsome as Father Inkersoll."

"I should get Davey first." Emer looked over to where her son sat conversing with the bishop as they both ate brown bread and cheese. Davey's speech was not too clear yet, but that never prevented him from having a lot to say.

Hazel chuckled. "Leave him be. My girls and Nancy's friend Beattie will look after him if Matt needs to do anything official." She sighed. "For all they're halflings, as you might say, our girls have *thrown hard to hob. Throw one, throw all*, is the way Matt likes to put it. He warned me when we were expecting our Nancy that if one of our children *threw hard,* the others would, too."

"How soon did you know?" Emer asked, fascinated. She thought Nancy, whom Hazel had pointed out as the eldest of the Charming daughters, might be conjuring if she'd started young, but the others probably wouldn't be able to do it yet.

Hazel took her arm, and they went to look at the gardens.

"I knew almost from the start. Nancy wouldn't settle

unless she was wrapped in enough blankets to stock a small draper's shop," Hazel said. She added, diffidently, "And what about your twins, Emer? Are they likely to take after their dad?"

"Andorie has his eyes, and Davey his hair-colour," Emer said.

"No, I meant . . ." Hazel's voice trailed off. "Oh dear, am I being impolite? I don't mean to be."

"Not at all! You're wishful to know if I'll have a brace o' kittens on my hands!" Emer chuckled at her new friend's expression. "Och, Hazel, we don't know, but it's not likely. Master Pendennis, who mentored my Rory in his mutie manners, has bairns, but he told me none has the manifest. It seems it pops up only every so often."

"Must be a recessive gene," Hazel said thoughtfully.

"That's the second time you've said that."

Hazel said, "Sorry. I wasn't showing off. Genes are the things in our physical make-up that dictate whether we'll be tall or short, or plump or slim. They say whether our eyes will be blue or brown."

"I did not know that," Emer said.

"Why should you? I only know it because I was a nurse when I met Matt. My brother studied medicine, and he used to bend my ear about *genes* and *chromosomes* and such. Mum thought all that talk was most unsuitable . . . but it was good practice for living with a hob. Matt's of the opinion, and I agree, that our girls should have the opportunity to do and be whatever they please, within the bounds of good sense. They visit with Matt's parents, and with mine, and already they're quite diplomatic in what they say to mine."

Emer wrinkled her forehead. "Your mam and dad *do* know Matt's fay?" She found it quite natural to use the bishop's given name. How could she not, when he was sharing bread and cheese with her son?

Hazel giggled. "They do, and they don't. They don't *want* to know. They choose to think he's an amiable eccentric . . . but he's a *bishop*, so they can scarcely suggest he's not eminently respectable. They're not at all religious, so they don't come to hear Matt preach. They get along all right, for all that."

"He's young for a bishop, surely." That was a stab in the dark, since Emer was unacquainted with any others, but Hazel nodded.

"And your husband is young for a priest. Matt's not quite as youthful as he looks, but he's a good deal younger than any other bishop in the other denominations around here. Somehow, his age has never been an issue for anyone."

Unlike Rory's. Emer hoped that thought didn't show on her face.

Hazel continued, "He wasn't a bishop when we met. He was the Reverend Mathias Charming. He'd been an army chaplain, but he was invalided out in nineteen forty-four after he got too close to an exploding mine. He'd been discharged from the hospital, but my brother visited him at home and gave him a physical. He suggested I might come to change the dressing. Matt had caught shrapnel in his shoulder, see. It'd been got out . . . Matt told me later he'd conjured it out himself . . . but it left a mess behind."

Emer divined she was talking of the war that had brought Kerry to spend more time *over there* with her leprechaun relations.

Hazel said, "Properly speaking, nurses aren't meant to fraternise with their patients, but I was just helping Jim out, so technically, Matt wasn't my patient."

"Oh. So you—"

"Jim had to spend a good deal of time unbundling Matt from multiple layers of clothing before he could look at the wound. Matt did *not* want to strip. I thought he must be bashful, being a reverend and all, but no — he just likes a lot of cloth. The wound was healing well — no infection, obviously, but it left a scar.

"I dressed it, but I could see it wouldn't need much attention. I told him that, but Matt said he had trouble reaching behind his shoulder with plaster and such."

Hazel caught Emer's puzzled expression and laughed. "Oh, of course, he could have conjured it, with or without using a mirror! To be fair, he did stop *just* short of lying over that. He said afterwards that he'd have lied like a trooper if he'd thought it was the only way to get me to visit him again. Jim was surprised at how often that wound seemed to need attention and he all but accused Matt of malingering. We had a good laugh over that when Matt finally broke the news that we'd decided to marry.

"So, Emer, how did you meet *your* lovely husband?"

"Och, he popped out at me when I was gathering wood and clawed up my skirts," Emer said.

Hazel choked.

Emer hastily explained.

"So, when you said you'd taught him baking when he was a child, you didn't mean you were children together," Hazel said.

"No, I'm much older than Rory. Twelve years."

"There are seven between Matt and me." Hazel sighed, and said pensively, "I never expected to marry a parson, let alone to become a bishop's wife! But once Jim introduced me to Matt, there was never anyone else for either of us. I'd have married him if he'd been as green as that leprechaun man lurking over there under the oak tree with the lady in the lovely peasant dress."

Emer chuckled. "That's my father-by-love, Lambert. The lady he's kissing is my mam, and she's wearing a traditional colleen's festival dress, no' a peasant dress."

"Oops! My mistake. And I should hope it's your mother if that's your stepfather . . . is that what you meant?"

"Aye." Emer decided not to explain the different permutations of the *by blood* and *by love* terminology as the leprechauns knew it. It was far too complex.

They continued with their walk through the gardens. These were serene and lovely, and Emer felt newly inspired to plant more flowers at the cottage. Since the twins' birth, she'd had time only for mostly functional plantings. "These are lovely," she said, gazing at a mixed border.

Hazel smiled. "I do a bit of weeding here now and then, and so do the parish ladies. But it's an odd thing . . . a lot of flowers grow out of season here. I could never make that out until Matt took pity on me and said it was the *wards . . .* whatever they are . . . that made this place *an annex of over there.*"

Emer nodded, understanding that. St Botolph's church was so near the gateway it was bound to be affected. She resolved to ask Rory if Master Grene had asked him to reinforce the wards. They must be rather precisely calculated to allow the human congregation to come and go without noticing the layers of protection.

Before they turned to go back inside the hall, Hazel put a hand on her arm.

"Emer . . . I hope you won't take this as interfering. It's meant as friendly advice. As I told you, Matt's been in the church for as long as I've known him. This is his third year as a bishop, but he was an army chaplain, as I said and then after we married, he was a parish parson for some years. He's a *giving* person, if you know what I mean."

Emer nodded cautiously.

"Your husband probably is, too. So maybe you might need to remind him now and then that he's a husband and a father first of all. He can't take care of the wider congregation if he's not caring for his family first. Matt has the balance perfectly, but I know of other parsons, good, kind men, whose wives and children seem to play second fiddle to their calling. That's not fitting, and it's not fair. Still, they're only human, I suppose. If you know what I mean."

"I do, and thank you . . . but it will be all right." Emer thought of how Rory loved her and the children and expanded that love to encompass others. "It was kind of you to say."

"I'm glad you didn't take offence. Listen, Emer. I know you won't have a telephone, but I think after you come to visit me at home the first time, that will mean you can conjure me a note if you need any help. That's right, isn't it?"

"I can't conjure through the gateway. Very few of us can."

"No-o, but you could step through. That's what Matt and his mum and dad do when they want to send messages to friends or relatives *over there*. And since Matt has been to visit Rory at your house, *he* could send you a note from me sometimes. If that wouldn't be intruding."

Emer thought about it. She'd not made lasting friendships during her time *over there*, because she'd never expected to make more than the occasional fleeting visit. Now she would be responsible for taking Flower to their cousin when the time came, and she knew she should come to the church sometimes to support Rory in his new role. Maybe it would be good to know a friendly human woman, especially one who knew Kerry, and who was at home with fay folk. And Hazel was fun, with her bubbly personality and her relish in telling a good story. Her little maids would be good for Andorie and Davey, who should get to know folk from other orders and humans, too.

She smiled. "Thank you, Hazel. I would like that fine. You would be welcome to bring the bairns to play with Davey and Andorie . . . are any of them old enough to open the gateway for you?" She recalled her supposition that Nancy might be able to conjure.

"Not yet. Matt says Nancy will probably be able to do it when she's eleven or twelve. Until then, Matt will let me through, or some of the other fay who *live human*. Not that Matt does that, exactly. He can seem human, or he can seem hob. It's as if there might be two of him."

There are two of Rory . . . counting the red cat. She knows about that, though.

They were still talking when Rory and Flower came looking for Emer. Rory had Andorie on his shoulders and Flower and the pisky girl had Davey by the hands.

"Beatrice!" someone called from the dispersing crowd walking through the gardens.

The pisky gave Flower an affectionate hug and ran off in a jingle of silver. If she *had* been using a glamour, she'd relaxed it after the service.

Flower said, "There ye are, Emer. I meant to come to ye sooner, but Beattie and I got to talking . . . Oh, and Mam says please, will ye come to see her wed again to Da."

Emer glanced over to the oak tree, where Lambert and Dornie were waiting for them. "Oh, yes. Is that today?"

"Da's taken a fancy to be back in Erin a' Fee before midsummer, so Rory's to say the words over them this afternoon."

"I see." Emer had known they were leaving, but she hadn't expected it so soon.

Hazel took her hand. "I know you have things to see to, Emer. I'll go and find the girls now. I hope to see you again soon."

"And I, you," Emer said. She meant it.

Hazel went off with a swing of sky-blue flowery skirts, and Emer went back to the gateway with her family and the Grenes. She was going to miss Flower, and so were the twins.

She'd miss Dornie, too, but this second leaving would seem less final, and besides, she had plenty of occupation with her husband and children. She would visit Catriona at the brae and call on Nairn McTavish to give her the family news. Nairn was a warm-hearted lassie. She would be pleased that Dornie would be wed again in the brae.

Yes, the family from Erin a' Fee must leave, but Emer had a new friend and much to look forward to.

CHAPTER TWENTY-TWO: DRY LAND WEDDING

January 1956, *The house at the brae*

Dornie and Lambert chose to be married at the house at the brae.

After returning the Grenes and Dorcas to the manse, the family walked there through the hazy midday sunshine.

The cottage was warm and welcoming, and the scent of baking hung around the porch. Bees hummed in the lavender. The scent of ripe strawberries sweetened the air in the garden. It was difficult for Emer to think of the cottage being empty again so soon.

Rory, unselfconscious in his cassock, with the sunlight striking sparks from his red hair, waited patiently while Lambert paced about, looking as nervous as if it was his first wedding and not his second to the same wife.

"What is it, Lambert?" Emer asked finally. She glanced at Dornie, who simply smiled and lifted her shoulders in an expressive shrug from her seat in a rocking chair on the porch.

Lambert O'Shea turned to Emer, half chagrined. "Darlin', I was seekin' the same spot I first laid eyes on your mam. I have a fancy to be wedded on that very spot. It seems fitting."

Emer thought back. "She was on the porch, I think, more or less where she is now."

"Ah! I see it! Ye were winding wool."

"So we were. And to see the porch, you must have been at

the gate there. That's where you were when we first saw *you*. You were just sliding off Fash's back, and we had no idea who you were or what you wanted until you came up and asked Mam to be yours."

He nodded with apparent relief. "That's the very place. I remember Fash got her tail caught on the latch and flicked me cheek getting it free. I barely noticed the sting, having caught sight of my darlin' to be."

"Then, now you have that firm in mind, do you think you might settle down and stop prowling and get yourselves wedded?"

He took her elbow and turned her about to speak privately. "I'm waitin' on the rings, Emer."

"You *have* wedding rings already," she reminded.

"Sure, sea-gold rings, kindly provided by the Master o' *Unicorn*, but this is our dry land wedding, see, and we need dry land rings to do it right."

"Does the Master of *Unicorn* keep a store of rings for unexpected weddings, then?"

"To be sure, darlin'. A lot o' the galleonfee captains do that. They're moral folk, and they hold great store in the proper union of man and maid."

"So they have rings at the ready! What a lovely idea!" Emer hugged her father-by-love impulsively.

"And now I'm supposin' ye'll do that, too, for those Rory might need to wed unexpectedly?" he asked in her ear.

The *sight*, which had been almost dormant since the twins were born, brought Emer a vision of a wooden box, carved and beautiful. In her mind's eye, she saw the brass hasp was loose, as if it had been unlocked only seconds ago. She opened the lid.

Inside, on a thick felt lining, lay a bewildering array of rings, twinkling in window-light from some future time. She smelled lemon verbena and herbs and the dear familiar scent of incense.

Oh, lovely . . .

She almost reached out to stir the silver and gold and gems with her fingertips, but then she heard Rory's voice. It was as clear as if he stood beside her, but oddly far away. She knew in an instant he was speaking out of the future and *the sight* had brought his voice back through the years for her to hear.

It *was* his voice, but he wasn't speaking to her.

Emer stilled herself to listen.

. . . my Emer, who has gone from me for now, was the love of my life. She was a practical braeside lassie, and she said no loving pair should be left wanting for rings. She had a great many made and wore them on a chain about her neck for a while to charm them. She said, you see, that she and I had enough love to spare and to share, and so they would be fit and ready for those who needed them.

No.

That was Emer's first thought, as a savage pang of dread and grief shot through her.

Her second thought came on its heels.

Calm down, you foolish lassie. You've always known you'd go to glory first, before Rory. You knew from that dreadful day, and you made Rory accept it. He won't be alone when you go. He'll have Davey and Andorie and perhaps others to love him. He'll always be loved. Always.

She held her hands in front of her, eyes closed, willing *the sight* to bring her something more.

Slowly, reluctantly, a new vision came. It showed her a red-headed man, much older than Rory, older than Lambert and Dornie, being hugged fiercely by a woman with black hair. A younger and very handsome man with black hair like the woman's and deep blue eyes had his arms around brown-haired women who were clearly twins. They were probably his sisters. She saw a beautiful woman with amber eyes that glinted with tears and a slightly younger one with strawberry blonde hair. She had one blue eye and one amber, and a mouth made for smiling

Who are they? Never mind. I'll know them in time. Show me my Rory.

Here he was, dressed in his cassock, with his collar she had embroidered so lovingly for his seventeenth birthday.

He still wears it?

He was gazing away from her, up into the sunlight. Oh, his hair was streaked heavily with grey, and the corners of his eyes creased with advancing years. He looked sad, but not distraught as he had been on *that* horrible day. He was her own dear Rory, still living in kindness and grace.

Da? Will you be all right when we've gone home to Erin a' Fee?

The woman with the mismatched eyes put her hand on his arm.

He turned to smile down at her. *Oh, Amber . . . yes, you know I'll be fine. I promised my queen long ago that I would go on in love. I never break my promises, especially to her. You go home to your lovelies and tell them —*

"Emer . . . Emer!"

Emer realised someone was shaking her. She opened her eyes and blinked, aware that tears lay on her cheeks. "Mam . . . stop it! I'll bite my tongue!"

"But, dearie, you were —"

"It was *the sight,* darlin', and it held her in thrall for a good while," Lambert said. He sounded shaken.

"Aye, that's all," Emer said mechanically. She drew a shuddering breath.

"And it's upset you."

She shook her head.

This is their wedding. I'll not spoil it with tears.

"It was a good thing to see. A happy thing. A long time off." As she spoke, she knew the words were true.

She staggered suddenly as Davey flung himself at her legs, and she reached down to gather him into her arms.

"Dog!" he yelped.

I saw you, oh, you were sixty years old! My Davey, with a black-haired love of your own to hold you.

She shook that memory away and kissed him. "What dog, laddie? Where's Dad?"

Davey pointed an emphatic finger over her shoulder.

Emer turned, hitching him onto her hip.

To her amusement, a roan spaniel dog was trotting smartly towards the cottage, grasping a cloth bag in its mouth. It spotted Rory and shied away from him, breaking into a lope before stopping in front of Lambert. It carefully dropped the bag at his feet and then sat back on its haunches, looking up expectantly.

Lambert, seeming nonplussed, stared at the bag. He reached out an uncertain hand towards the dog.

Don't pat him, oh, Lord save us . . . do not touch his ears.

Lambert appeared to change his mind, for he withdrew his hand.

The dog gave a yip that sounded like a laugh and unfolded into the pisky man, Jago Pendennis. "Pick it up, man! I thought you were in a hurry to wed your lovely here?" he asked. He turned to Dornie and bent to kiss her cheek. "Mistress, is your man always so—"

"Green?" Lambert suggested, recovering himself.

Flower, holding Andorie by the hand, goggled at him. "Who in the world . . ."

Emer perceived someone had to do something. She couldn't look at Rory yet, not so soon after seeing him bereaved and aging, so she set Davey on his feet and busied herself with sorting out the situation.

"Master Jago, have you brought the rings for Mam and Lambert?"

"So I have. I promised Master O'Shea he'd have them in time. Gold, too." He sounded somewhat disapproving.

Emer knew that most piskies loved silver and worked gold only as an afterthought or a commission. Leprechauns, on the other hand, favoured gold rings. Unsurprisingly, they loved emeralds, jade and other green gemstones.

She watched Lambert pick up the bag before grasping the pisky man's hand. "Pardon me for gawkin', Master Pendennis. I was niver expectin' the rings to be delivered by a—a—"

"His dog self's name is Master Floppy," Emer said. She smiled at the pisky, seeing honours were just about even. "Master, I need to have a few words with you someday soon. Is it all right if I call on you and your lady at Treborrow to tell you about it?"

"You're welcome any time, and Emblyn will be pleased to offer tea." He glanced sharply at Rory. "Bring the red cat with you. Our elder miss, Chesten, and *her* miss, Beatrice, are staying with us for a while, and will want to meet him properly," he said.

"Oh! Emer, can I come, too, and see Beattie—" Flower stopped short. "But I won't be here," she added woefully.

"I'll bring him," Emer promised the pisky man.

To Flower, she said, "When you're back to stay with Kerry, maybe you and Beatrice can get together then."

"It's such a long time to wait." Flower sighed.

Master Jago nodded to Emer. "Very good. Now, I'm off back to my minx and our misses. Rory can get on with the job of wedding these fine folk. Fare you all well." He raised a hand and bowed to them all impartially. Then he dissolved again into the roan spaniel. It trotted jauntily away, its plumy tail high and wagging with the wellbeing of a job well done.

Emer stared after him. Evidently he was pleased to have his daughter and grandchild to visit. It was a pity Flower had to leave behind a just-made friend, but then, was there ever a good time to leave a friend?

I wish they could be here for good and all . . . Och, but that's selfish. Cormac and Dervla will be missing them sorely, and so will Fash and Glory-Be.

She turned as her father-by-love touched her shoulder.

"Darlin' Emer, will you and Flower stand up for us as witnesses?"

"Oh, of course." She looked about for the twins and located them in the strawberry bed, where they must have gone while she was dealing with Master Floppy. She supposed they wouldn't be very surprised, since their own father sometimes manifested as the red cat. She wrinkled her brow. It was a while since she'd had the chance to sit contemplatively with her purring, furry consolation in her lap.

She took Flower's hand, and they went to stand with Dornie and Lambert at the gateway where they had first laid eyes on one another fifteen years before.

Emer realised Flower was almost to her shoulder. That meant she'd be tall for a colleen, though otherwise a true-to-see type.

Rory took up his stance before the group. If he was nervous about performing his first official wedding, it didn't show.

He began, with no preliminary throat clearing. "Dornie and Lambert, you two chose one another many years ago. You decided then to walk together into your forever. Are you still of that same mind?"

"We are," they said together as if they had rehearsed it.

"And will you continue to be the support and comfort of one another for as long as you both live?"

"We will." Dornie smiled.

"And will you continue to take joy in one another, and in your family, as the Lord intends it?"

"We will," Dornie said.

"We *do*," Lambert added.

"In that case, you should exchange rings," Rory said, smiling at them.

There was a pause while Lambert, who, as a traditional green gossoon, didn't conjure, removed the ring pouch from the breast of his tunic where he'd stowed it. If it was wet with spaniel-spit, he showed no distaste but pulled open the draw-string.

He and Dornie slipped on the gold pisky-crafted rings, slim and studded with green and purple stones to reflect the green way and the braeside. They fitted perfectly, as Jago Pendennis's rings always seemed to do. No doubt that practical pisky charmed the things to fit.

Rory said, "I pronounce you now and forever, in the presence of witnesses, as husband and wife in the eyes of the Lord. You may do whatever is seemly before your daughters' eyes."

Lambert caught Dornie around the waist and whirled her about, kissing her soundly. Then he picked up Flower and spun her as well. He thrust her to her mother and threw his arms around Emer and Rory.

"Oh, ye've made me a happy man, darlin's! 'twas the best dry-land wedding ever two folk had."

"Don't you have to bless them?" Emer asked breathlessly.

Rory spluttered with laughter. "I do. Settle down, my dear children."

What? Emer stared at him, but Lambert dropped to his knees and pulled Dornie down beside him.

Rory put a hand on each of their heads and commended their happiness to the Lord and to one another. Then he stepped back and put an arm around Emer. He whispered, "Do you think we should invite Flower back with us for the night?"

"Why—oh, yes. Let's."

Emer had been looking forward to celebrating the ordination in the best way, but she saw her mother and father-by-love also had something to celebrate, and fewer years in which to do it. They were both in their middle-fifties by now. She turned to Flower. "Hen, would you like to come home with us and pile in with the twins for the night?"

Flower, looking subdued, nodded. "I'll get them out of the

strawberries."

She went to do so and then they took their leave of the new-lyweds and headed back to the pixie forest cottage. On the way, Flower said suddenly, "Rory, *deartháir darbh ainm?*"

"Hmm? What is it, dear sister-by-love?"

"When I make my gossoon mine, will you say the words for us the way ye did for Da and Mam?"

Emer recollected she'd heard no more of Flower's gossoon since her first days with them, more than two years before. Flower had never again raised the subject, and neither had Elmer, dismissing it as a child's fancy. Now, with her sister leaving so soon, she couldn't believe she'd never even asked the laddie's name.

"But—you'll be wed in Erin a' Fee, surely, when the time comes," she said. *If the time comes,* she corrected herself mentally. Not all leprechauns bothered to marry, although they were devoted and faithful lovies.

"If so, Rory can come to us. You, too, Emer, and the twins. Or maybe we'll all come to you. I should like to introduce you to my own gossoon." She seemed to be calculating something, for she added, "Emer, if you have your next babby in around three or four years, then I can be here to use my *loving touch* on your back. And I can bring my gossoon, and Rory can wed us then." She switched her attention back to Rory. "Will ye do that, *deartháir darbh ainm?*"

Rory glanced at Emer. She shrugged, and then she said, "If you and your gossoon come, Flower, we'll have rings waiting for you. By the by . . . what's yon laddie's name?"

"Thank you." Flower gave a jerky nod and took Davey and Andorie by the hands. "Ye're all sticky wid the strawberry juice, darlin's. Let's run down to the falls an' let the waterfolk splash wid ye."

The twins clamoured their acceptance of this notion, and they hurried off with their aunt.

"Och, what in the world was that about?" Emer said.

"I suspect your sister has set her mind on a lad and has yet to inform him. He could be from another village, or maybe from that greenway island you mentioned, so they've not been correctly introduced."

"Bodhran Island," she said, remembering. "Rory, no one lives there. I believe there are some leppies on the Isle o' Samhradh, though. Or perhaps Flower has gone to a ceilidh on Bodhran. She's far too young to have gone to the love village, but she might have fallen for a fine pair of green eyes."

"What's the love village?" Rory asked.

"*Sráidbhaile an Ghrá*, it's called, a lovely place with thyme and white cottages. Mam and Lambert went there for a while when Flower was a wee lassie. I looked after her while they were gone."

Rory stared after his sister-by-love and his children and changed the subject.

Emer thought that fair enough, since the mystery was, for now, impenetrable.

"My queen, how long does it take to remove strawberry juice and good soil and compost from two scamps?"

"Quite a while, if Flower gets talking with the water maids. You know how the twins love splashing with the waterfolk. And they could not be in kinder or safer hands," she said.

"I suggest we go home and get some rest before they return for tea or, better still, for supper."

"Rest, is it?"

Rory's smile lit up the world. "My darling queen, whatever it is, I think we should do it lying down. It's been a busy day."

CHAPTER TWENTY-THREE: CATS' EYES

February 1956, *The Cottage*

Rory must have known Emer missed the family when they'd left on the galleonfee ship bound for Erin a' Fee, for he was especially loving to her and to the twins.

Davey and Andorie were both inclined to be woeful. They loved their aunt dearly, and so Emer found she was indulging them a little more than was wise. But then, so was Rory.

Emer loved the extra attention he gave her, but she felt guilty about allowing it to continue. She said, gently, "There's no need to coddle me, dear laddie. I know fine they'll be back in a year. In the meantime, Cormac and Dervla can enjoy their company. They deserve to."

"Especially if they've been caring for Fash," Rory said with a chuckle. He was threading amethyst crystals on a fine wool thread, and she watched his deft fingers as he tied a knot and chose a new piece of stone. He had long hands, so beautifully shaped she thought he might have been a full-time artist, had he not had a different calling.

But then, in his way, he was.

She watched him for a while until the crystals blurred. Rory held up the finished string, and a late ray of sunlight struck it and shattered into a glittering cross.

Emer jumped as she saw a strange couple just beyond the cross. For a moment, she thought the man was Matt Charming, but he was too young, and the woman was a buxom hob maid with fair hair and a full smock decorated with corn and forget-me-not embroidery.

Have you brought rings, Jem?

That was Rory's voice . . . the voice she thought of as *Father Inkersoll.*

Aye, and we'll trouble you to get t' words said smart, like . . . afore . . .

Jem! Be seemly! That was the hob maid, laughing and glowing with joy.

The voices and the vision faded and Emer took a deep, steadying breath.

She realised Rory was staring at her, over the crystal string. "Are you all right, my queen?"

"Och, yes . . . yes. Rory, you need to make a crystal cross. Or at least, you need to get one, somehow."

He gave her a quizzical look. "Why, would you like one?"

"No . . . at least, aye, if you wanted me to wear one. I meant, a big one, half the size of a man, fine enough to catch and spatter the light."

He laid down the amethysts and reached for her hands. "Emer, what's this about?"

The words fell out in a scramble. "You'll have one by you sometime. I don't know when, but a hob couple will come to be wed, and there will be a crystal cross. The man is called Jem. The maid will have fair hair, and they'll be in an uncommon hurry to be wed."

"A typical enough name for a hob man, and a lot of them are fair, but as for a hob in a hurry, is such a thing possible?"

Emer squeezed his hands. "I cannot tell you anything more."

"I'll go to Jago and see what crystals he can spare," Rory said equably. He lifted her hands to his lips. "So, *the sight* has come back to you? Just now?"

"It's shown me some things, lately," she said, troubled.

"Not a tall lassie riding away from me on that dratted kelpie mare, I trust. I give you fair warning. If that creature ever comes for you again, she'd better be feeling strong, because she'll be carrying four of us."

"I promise you I have not seen that. If I go back to Erin a' Fee, it will be sailing with the fair winds fleet, and with you and the twins for company." Then, trying for a lighter air, she added, "But I thought you liked Fash? You spent some time colluding with yon kelpie when she took me away and again when she fetched me home."

Rory sighed. "That wasn't me. It was the red cat that fiend of a mare liked. When she saw me in my man form, the wretch tried to bite me. I gave her oatcake, and she almost took my finger with it. It was deliberate, all snaking head and flashing eyes. She gave me to understand she liked me well enough in fur, but otherwise—no. She could not be doing with me."

"You never told me that so plainly before."

"Believe me. I had more on my mind than an almost-bitten finger when I saw you again, my queen."

"Rory, you were only sixteen." That fact still made her uncomfortable.

"Seventeen come summer," he said, as he had back then. "And now I'm twenty-one, and I have never been happier." He rose from his chair, drew her to her feet, put her arms around her and said in her ear, "I'm almost afraid of how deeply happy I am. I'm surrounded by so much love."

Emer shivered, remembering the vision *the sight* had given her on the day of his ordination and Dornie and Lambert's dry land wedding. "You'll always be surrounded by love, darling laddie. *Always.*"

He pulled her closer. "I always have been, although I didn't always realise. Mum loved me, and when she went to glory, I had a lot of kindness from Berry and Mistress Clover. They never treated me as a son, because that wasn't what I needed. I wasn't a pixie, after all. They let me become what I was going to be, and they did it with grace."

"They are good folk," she said awkwardly.

"Jago and Emblyn made me welcome in their home, and young Peter G . . . he brought me back from a bleak place of my own making. And then there was you. I've had you now for longer than I was without."

And there will be me for as long as I can contrive.

The haunting memory came back. Rory, with his brilliant hair darkened and streaked with grey, still kind, still loving, and still surrounded by love.

And me not there.

She focused on those folk *the sight* had shown her. Davey, a man in his sixties, had a dark-haired love. Andorie had been alone, but beautiful. The dark young man might be her own grandson, and the serene brown-haired twins were probably her grandchildren, too. And there was that lovely marmalade-haired woman, with the odd-coloured eyes. Amber, Rory had called her.

They are my family. And me not there.

She said, "You were ten when we met, and eleven years have passed since then. But Rory, I was gone in Erin a' Fee for close to two of those."

"You were in Erin a' Fee, but you were never *gone*. I always knew I'd see you again and then we'd have our forever."

Forever.

She pressed herself against Rory so urgently he dropped his face to give her a passionate kiss.

Aye, take away the sorrow. Let me forget.

She kissed him back and pulled away to say, *"please . . ."*

Rory lifted his head. "Where are the twins?"

"Looking for beetles in the bean patch."

"God bless the beetles," Rory said. He led her into their bedroom, conjured the door closed and had them both bare in an instant.

They dropped together onto their bed, and Emer reached for the spread to cover them.

"No, let me look at you," Rory said.

Emer rolled onto her back, and he got up on his elbows. His amber gaze moved slowly over her body, and she watched his eyes widen and darken. She held out her arms.

"Come to me. You can look any time, *any* time."

"I want to remember this moment, just as you are," he murmured.

Emer quivered. "If you look much longer, you'll see something most unseemly. Your wife will melt into a puddle of longing, and it won't be pretty."

He gave a breathless laugh and rolled on top of her.

A few minutes later, they were still joined and floating on a warm sea of fulfilment. Rory said, "I meant it when I said I want to remember you just as you are. I want to remember this best year, and the best thing in it."

Emer nipped his ear and said tartly, "I hope that doesn't mean you plan to spend hours each day staring at my naked body."

"Not *hours* . . . but . . ." He kissed her chin and wriggled down to kiss her breast, rubbing his cheek against her.

Emer could gladly have stayed there all day, but she knew the twins would soon have finished pursuing beetles. They would be wanting soda bread and apples.

Presently, she conjured on her gown and pinned up her hair. "Rory." She examined herself in a pier-glass Hazel had given her when she remodelled her sitting room. She found him looking back at her from the bed.

"Yes, I remembered to *hold,*" he said, smiling.

"Not that. I wondered if you've ever seen any person with different coloured eyes. Different from one another, I mean."

To her surprise, he nodded. "Do you remember I told you Mum had a kind of cousin named Corrie?"

"Aye, she's a colleen, you said."

"That's right. I'm not too sure how they were related, but

Corrie would know."

"And?"

He looked surprised. "You asked — oh, I see. Corrie has eyes the way you said, two different colours."

"What colours are they?"

He pondered. "It's years since I saw her, but I know one was the same colour as mine because Mum said I looked more like Corrie than like her. Corrie has red hair, too, though it's much lighter than mine. More like a marmalade cat. Mum had brown hair, going grey, and hazel eyes." His face shadowed. "I wish I had a picture of Mum, so I could show you and the twins."

"Maybe you could draw one," she suggested.

She wondered why he never had. He'd drawn many portraits of her and the children.

"Maybe I will. It might take a while to bring her back to mind, though." He stretched, and Emer watched the ripple of muscles as the movement shifted from his fingertips to his toes. For a moment, his eyes changed, the pupils narrowing to upright slits. He froze, and he looked disconcerted. Then he put his hands briefly over his eyes.

Emer turned away from the glass and came back to sit beside him on the bed. "Rory, I haven't seen Red in a good while."

"No," he said quietly. He dropped his hands. His eyes were back to normal.

"Is there any reason?"

"Other than I am so happy in my skin that I don't want to miss a moment of being me?"

"Other than that."

He sat up. "I suppose I associate the red cat with times of uncertainty. If you remember, I used to sink myself into that state whenever the world or temptation was too much for me. Do you recall when we first kissed?"

How could I forget?

137

"It was four years and two months ago," she said.

"Only that long? It feels forever ago to me. Before it happened, I warned you I might need to be the red cat, after."

"I remember that, but you stayed you."

"I wanted to go on feeling everything with you, even though it was so difficult to contain. That was the first time I held the red cat at bay instead of giving in to him."

Something cold laid its fingers on Emer's heart. She said slowly, choosing her words, "I do not think you should do that to Red. Hold him back, I mean. He needs to *be*, and he needs to be loved, just as you do."

Rory opened his mouth, and his chin went stubborn.

Emer put her fingers over his lips. "No, hear me out, please. I quite see it would be disconcerting if Red appeared while you were taking a service, for example, or while you were visiting a human parishioner, or baptising a child. But here at home with us, he should be given his share of the sun."

He made another attempt to speak, but she went on, "Red is my dear friend. He was my comfort when *I* had soul-cold. I love you more than I can possibly say, but I hate to think of Red being made unhappy for our convenience. It's so long since he played with the twins, or snuggled on my lap, or rolled in the herb patch in the sun. He didn't even have the chance to say his farewells to Flower."

She took her hand away from her husband's mouth and waited with some apprehension on what he might say.

To her astonishment, he caught her in his arms and rolled her down on the bed, pushing his face under her chin.

"Rory, what are you doing?"

He stopped. "Thanking you for being *you*, my queen, and for giving me a better direction. You're quite right. I just realised how *I* would feel if the red cat took up all your attention. I'd be cold and starved. I've been unkind and unfair to him, and it will never happen again. *Never*."

He kissed her and jumped up from the bed, conjured on his clothing and helped her to her feet.

Then he gave her his brilliant smile and went out into the kitchen. After a few seconds, she heard a delighted squeal from Andorie.

She made sure her clothing was properly adjusted and put the kettle on the hob. She measured tea into the pot and then went out into the garden to find her children lying in her camomile patch, twirling daisy flowers for the red cat.

CHAPTER TWENTY-FOUR: EMBLYN

March 1956, *Treborrow*

A few weeks after Dornie and Lambert's departure, Emer went to Treborrow to visit Jago and Emblyn Pendennis.

Rory escorted her there, saying he had business with the pisky jeweller. This business concerned the crystal cross Emer had seen in her vision. Jago professed himself intrigued with the idea, and he and Rory went off to the workroom to talk about materials and methods of creating such a thing.

Emer was left in the kitchen with the twins and Emblyn Pendennis.

She had met Jago's formidable minx before, at their wedding, and at other times, but only briefly. She was disconcerted when Emblyn fixed her brilliant hazel gaze on the twins and brushed her hands together in a clatter of silver bracelets. "You, twins. Take a pail each. Go out into the garden. Pick peas. Eat peas, too, but no more than one in every handful of pods. I'll know if you disobey." She clapped her hands. "What are you waiting for? Spit spot!"

The twins exchanged astonished glances with Emer and one another, and then Davey picked up two child-sized pails that had popped into sight by the door.

He handed one to Andorie, and he and his sister left in silence.

Emer half-opened her mouth to protest, but Emblyn Pendennis turned and winked at her, her haughty expression dissolving into a mischievous grin.

"That was unpardonable of me, I know, but I wanted to see if I could still do it. Don't worry, Mama, they'll come to no harm. My man has excellent hearing, and at the first sign of trouble, he'll be there to lick them into submission."

"I see," Emer said. She wondered how Mistress Pendennis would feel if she began ordering *her* children about. But of course, they were grown. Even their son, Truro, who was a few years Rory's junior, might by now have enough years to be courting some lovely miss. He, too, would be beyond his mother's say-so.

I hope for everyone's sake any maid Truro loves is a strong-minded lassie.

Emblyn conjured tea things to the table. "I see you've brought oatcakes for us. My man makes them. I believe they began as your recipe, taught to him by your Rory, but he's added a few touches. I'll be happy to try some of yours." She sat down to pour tea and said brightly, "My, it's good to talk to another mutie bride."

"Och, I'm no mutie," Emer said, startled.

"No, dear, and neither am I. But we're both wed to one, and so we're both overly familiar with the paws and claws and whiskers aspects . . . and the tongues, oh, the tongues! Like a yard of red flannel in hot weather. Not to speak of that interesting smell of wet dog in the rain.

"So, how is the red cat faring now Rory's been priested?"

"He's well," Emer said. She was still trying to process that extraordinary speech.

The pisky woman nodded approval. "I'm glad to hear it. My man was concerned when he saw Rory last."

Emer said, "Was that when Master Jago brought the rings for Mam and Lambert's dry land wedding?"

"Just so."

"That was the same day Rory was ordained," Emer said.

"I know. Naturally, we were in church to see it happen. No, you didn't see us, and that's down to Jago, and not to any neglect on your part. We were at the back of the church with our miss, Chesten, and Beatrice. The misses stayed on for the reception because Beatrice was taken with your sister. Jago and I came back early . . . Jago had those rings to charm in a hurry, and he had me put on your mother's to imbue it with what he calls *an aura of wifely happiness*. My Jago has a high opinion of his ability to inspire wifely happiness."

She pushed a butter dish towards Emer. "Try this butter. I get it from a colleen at Crock o' Gold. She adds something to it, some herb or other, but blessed if I know what. I could probably compel her to tell me, but then, a colleen has as much right to her secrets as a pisky minx or even a braeside lassie."

She watched as Emer buttered an oatcake and then went on, "Rory looked good to me that day, lit up inside and out. He's a fine man and a fine pastor. I've nothing but motherly affection for him, *but* I don't pretend to see what Jago sees."

Emer looked at her, puzzled, and still trying to catch up with the flood of talk. Emblyn Pendennis did bounce from subject to subject.

Emblyn said, "It's a mutie thing. You know Master Floppy, obviously."

"Aye."

Emblyn's grin came back. "He's a wonder, that dog. Despite the tongue and the wet dog smell, I love him to bits. He's my cuddle friend. Sometimes when Jago's being more than usually aggravating, I tell him straight that I want to spend a day or so with Master Floppy. He's as warm-hearted, clever, and devoted as Jago, but he's also *quiet*, which Jago is not.

"You know how it is, I'm sure. The red cat's a mite more restful than Rory, no doubt. Unlike Master Floppy, he won't drool on your feet when you're eating cheese. He also won't wrap his tongue around the back of your ankle."

Emer choked.

142

"There now, I got a smile out of you." The pisky woman drank her tea in one long draught. "See, Jago can perceive the red cat in some way even when Rory's in man-form. Only as a shadow, he says. Master Floppy, on the other hand, sees the cat as clear as I see you."

She took a deep breath and puffed out her cheeks, shaking back her grey-streaked hair so her short silver earring jingled. That style of earring, as Emer knew, denoted a pisky man or woman devoted and fulfilled with a *forever* match.

Emblyn went on, "And after he gave those rings over to your ma and her gossoon, Jago came back to me and said Master Floppy had spotted that the red cat was a mite more shadowy than he ought to be."

"Why didn't he say something to us? Master Pendennis, I mean?" Emer asked.

"He did. He laid it on you to *bring the red cat* to visit. That's plain enough, surely."

"I'm afraid I was a wee bit distracted that day," Emer said.

"That's clear, since you turned up with the man-form. But all's well with the red one now, right?"

"Yes. I think so. I hope so. How did you know that?"

"*I* don't, but Jago does. He gave me the nod as soon as he saw Rory. The cat's back, in fine fettle, and let me warn you right now, if that creature tries to whisker swipe *me*, I'll send him spit-spat. I did it before, and I'm more than willing to do it again. Master Floppy's the only fur-folk who may claim *me*. And so you may tell him."

She nodded emphatically and said, "Right, I've said my piece, and I'm glad it wasn't much needed. If you want to call your twins in, you do it. I hope you see why I sent them out. I did *not* want to discuss these things with those children close at hand. They're much too knowing and much too aware for whatever age they are. Clearly, they get their intelligence from *both* of you. One clever parent's never enough to give

143

you clever children. *I* know."

"I'm sure they're happy picking peas," Emer said. She loved to hear the twins being praised, even in such a backhanded manner, because she was sure Emblyn Pendennis always said just what she happened to think.

Emblyn turned out to be good company, and Emer was surprised to find herself reminded of her new friend, Hazel Charming. Had she been able to get more than a few words in edgeways, she might have asked if Emblyn knew the bishop's wife well. Then she reflected it might be better to ask Hazel.

Emblyn was still talking volubly when the men came in. Rory had Davey on his hip, and the Pendennis granddaughter, Beatrice, had Andorie by the hand. In her other hand, the girl carried two pails bursting with fat pea pods.

Emer noticed Beatrice had bright eyes and a determined chin like her grandmother's. She was a handsome child, in the pisky manner, with curling fair hair and pointed ears.

"Have the twins been bothering you, Beatrice?" she asked.

Beatrice shook her head. "I was happy to see them, Mistress Inkersoll. How's Flower? Have you heard from her?"

"Aye, they've arrived home safe to Erin a' Fee," Emer said.

Rory put in, "Flower asked me to give you this, Beattie." He took a much-folded letter from his pouch. "She would have sent it to you directly, but —"

"But she's never been to where I live, or even to Granny and Grandad Pendie's," Beatrice said. She waved away Rory's attempt to hand over the letter. "I want to try and conjure it from your hand to mine, Father Rory. May I?"

Rory smiled. "You know how?"

"Just about."

She fixed her bright gaze on him. "Your cat's handsome. I'd like to stroke it."

Rory blinked, and his eyes narrowed. He shut them for a

moment, and Emer saw his hand close tightly on the letter. Then he visibly relaxed. He smiled. "Thank you. I take it that means you can see him right now?"

The child nodded. "Mm. I can. I can see Grandad's Master Floppy, too. Shall I tell you what he's doing?"

"Yes, if your grandad doesn't mind," Rory said.

"Go ahead," Jago said. He sounded proud of his grand-daughter's ability.

Beatrice turned her gaze to her grandfather. "He's asleep in a patch of barley straw, with his paws in the air. He's happy because the sun's warming his belly." She turned back to Rory. "Your cat's awake, though. He's looking back at me and doing that slow-blink." She directed her gaze floorwards and wiggled her fingers in invitation.

"In that case, you should conjure your letter right away so he can come out to play," Rory said equably.

Beatrice lifted her bright gaze to his face and held out both hands. *"Come."*

A second later, Emer heard the crackle of paper, and the girl waved her letter triumphantly. "Got it! And unfolded, too! Ooh, Flower's sent me a drawing of the kelpie mare! Thank you, Father Rory."

"You're welcome, Beattie." Rory smiled and dropped into the red cat.

"Red," Emer said gladly. She held out her hand, and Red scrubbed his cheek against her knuckles. He purred and then turned his amber gaze on Emblyn Pendennis.

He flicked his tail and advanced on the pisky woman.

Immediately, Emblyn made that dusting gesture with her hands. "Spit—" Before she could get the last word out, Red chirruped and flicked his tail again before swaggering over to the twins.

Emer sighed and turned to Beatrice. "Lassie, if you'd like to reply to Flower, I'd be happy to send it on to her."

"Of course. Father Rory can't do that, can he?"

"No, because he's never been to Erin a' Fee."

Beatrice nodded. "I understand. I think I'll send her a drawing, too. If I'm not here when you leave, please send it anyway."

"You're going somewhere?" Emer asked.

"Yes. Grandma's going to take me to see Nancy. That's Nancy Charming. She and I are *particular friends.*" She pursed her lips and added, "I would like to be *particular friends* with Flower, too, but she's a long way from here. Can you be friends with someone if you don't get to see her often?"

"I'm sure you can," Emer said, thinking of Lambert, Dornie, Flower and Lambert's mam and da. "You can hold them in your heart until you meet again."

Beatrice smiled and then tucked away her letter. Then she fell on her knees by the twins. She held out her hand to Red, waiting with good manners until he had finished cheek-bumping the twins.

Red chirruped and dropped his head so she could rub behind his shoulders.

"You look well, red cat," Emblyn said. She held up a finger and beckoned Beatrice back to her feet. "Off you go, miss. Spit-spat!"

Chapter Twenty-five: Rings

March 1956, *Treborrow*

The girl got up obediently and went off to write and draw her letter. Red and the twins went out into the garden, and Emblyn told her man that Master Floppy should go with them.

Emer waited apprehensively for another outpouring of opinion and advice, but it seemed that Emblyn had said everything she intended. She veered off into talk of recipes, quilts and gardens, topics on which Emer could easily hold her own.

After a while, she called to Beatrice and announced it was time they went to the gateway for the proposed visit with Nancy Charming.

"I'd invite you along since I know you and Hazel are friends, but you have business with my man."

"So I have," Emer said.

"We'll leave you to it, then. When you're ready, blow this whistle, and the old dog will come in. Beattie, give your letter to Mistress Inkersoll, now. She'll see it on its way directly."

Beatrice gave Emer a letter sealed with red wax, stamped with her monogram, an emphatic capital B. Emer noted a cool, sweet smell of jasmine, which was the girl's personal scent. Emblyn smelled of catnip, as her husband had once commented, so it wasn't so surprising that her granddaughter had a floral scent.

Emer smiled in acknowledgement. She held the letter in her lap, picturing Flower's whitewashed bedroom at the cottage in Erin a' Fee. The quilt she and Dornie had worked on, made up in the leprechaun design of horseshoes and shamrock, but with sprigs of brae-heather pieced in, would be spread over the blanket. The letter from Beatrice would be resting on the pillow when Flower went into her room.

There.

Oh, I love you, my sister of my heart.

Beatrice thanked her politely and assured Emer she would also thank Father Rory. Then she went off with her grandmother.

As she left, the Pendennis kitchen blurred around Emer. She felt herself sway on the upright chair. A figure stepped into being before her. The woman looked to be close to twenty. She had a determined chin, and she was hung with silver charms and bindings in the pisky manner. She held a pisky earring in her hands and appeared to be in the act of hooking a catch to it.

That's the way they adapt an earring when they make a commitment. She should look happy. Why doesn't she look happy?

The woman raised her face from the task and looked directly at Emer. Tears trembled in her eyes.

Glory be, it's Beattie!

The sight faded, leaving Emer alone in the kitchen. She sat for a while, letting the silence wash over her.

What can Beattie have to do with me? The sight never shows me anything irrelevant.

The only thing that came to mind was that Beattie was Flower's friend. The girl had wanted to be Flower's *particular friend.*

Dear Lord, I hope she's not wanting to bed with Flower. By the time she has enough years, Flower will have said forever *with her gossoon.*

There was nothing she could do about any of that. Not yet, at any rate. Emer commended her uncertainty to the Lord. Rory had taught her to do that, and while she had not the strength of devoted faith that sustained her husband, Emer felt that at least the Lord and she understood one another. Both of them loved Rory. They wanted the best for him.

When she felt ready, she picked up the whistle Emblyn had indicated. It was made from sweetwood, she saw, and beautifully carved. It fitted in her hand as if intended for her use, and it gave her a strange feeling of kinship.

Charmed, obviously.

She raised it to her lips and blew, unsurprised when a single sweet note modulated into a chord. She wasn't particularly musical, although Rory was. His spirited performances on the pipes often had her and the twins dancing until they were breathless.

She laid the whistle aside with a reluctance that surprised her.

It's not yours, silly lassie. Not to do with you. Not directly.

Seconds later, the door shivered and swung slightly open. The roan spaniel, Master Floppy, nudged it the rest of the way with his long nose. Emer perceived he had depressed a lever with his paw to open the door.

"Red can go right through walls and doors," she said.

Master Floppy unfolded into the pisky jeweller. "That's because he's a stealth cat mani. Took us a while to sort that out, since Master Floppy can't do it." He sat down in one of the straight-backed chairs. "You had something to discuss with me, Rory's queen?"

"Aye. Where are Rory and the twins?"

"They've gone along with my minx and Beatrice, as far as the pixie forest. Rory said he'd put the children to bed for a nap at home. So?"

Emer said, "Master Jago, I wanted to talk to you about rings."

He smiled. "Not surprised. That's what most folk talk to me about. You and Rory want another pair?"

"Och, no!" Emer examined her ring with the ambers and

mother-of-pearl. It had done duty as kissing ring, betrothal ring and now was her wedding ring. "This one is perfect, and I'll never need another."

"First kiss till last," the pisky said, nodding his understanding.

"Aye, and a great many in between."

He laughed. "Many, many more than most folk manage, I expect. Same as with my minx and me."

"We're lucky, all four of us. The rings I want to ask about are for others. You know Mam and my father-by-love had wedding rings already."

"Island gold. Good work, as far as gold goes. Thought the gossoon wanted to get good silver when he poked his green nose around my workshop door. No, more gold was what he had in his mind."

"He wanted new rings for their dry land wedding." Emer repeated what Lambert had told her about the genesis of the island gold rings.

Jago nodded. "Then I'm all ahead of you, Rory's queen. You've taken the notion to have rings ready for any hasty wedding Rory might want to perform down the years."

"That's it." Emer laid two fingers on her own dear ring. "I'd like to get a great many, Master Jago. Some could be silver, and others might be gold, or copper, or even sweetwood. I've seen the work you do . . . Mistress Emblyn has lovely rings, and the two you made for Mam and Lambert were fine. But it's no' just the craftmanship I want, but the love you put in them."

Jago raised one eyebrow. "Come, Rory's queen, you know what they say about piskies."

"Jealous, self-serving, manipulative and pigheaded," Emer said as if reciting a lesson.

"Exactly so."

"But you're no' like that."

"Oh, I am," he said with a grim smile. "I'm a pisky man, sure as you're a braeside lassie with *the sight*. You *know* what I am."

Emer leaned forward. "I know that I *will* have those rings. I'm guessing when I think they'll come from you."

"Well, Rory's queen . . . did you ever discover why he calls you that?"

"It's to do with Red, I think. Red's a tom, and she-cats are queens. And *you* may say you're a hard-headed pisky man all you like, master, but I see different. You and Mistress Emblyn gave Rory love when he needed it. There was nothing in that for you. You two had your own children. You didn't need to school a redheaded changeling. Still, you did, and then later you came to give me advice of your own will. Emblyn gave me some, too, just now. You two are good, kind folk, no matter how you care to pretend otherwise."

The jeweller said, "I blame that dratted dog. He queers my mind and turns me sentimental."

"He does not. He *is* you, in a way. He's a dear creature. He couldn't be that if you weren't. Is he satisfied with Red's health now?"

"Who's been talking out of turn?"

"Never mind that. Is he?"

"The red cat's as smug and smarmy as a cat should be. Ask Beattie if you don't believe me."

"I believe you. Is Beattie a mutie, too?"

The mournful face *the sight* had given her swam back into her vision, and she put it aside.

"Not as far as I can judge. Chesten and Penzance aren't, and neither's Truro. Emblyn's big boy Enyon wouldn't have been in any case. His father is a man of the pisky hills. Chesten's man Perren's not, so likely Beattie won't be either. Muties are more commonly men, and it often hops generations."

"Oh?"

"Don't ask *me* why. Mistress Charming may have an answer for you. She said something of *sex-linked genes* to Emblyn. Quite put my minx to the blush. Takes a lot to do that."

Emer put that aside as well to be considered later. "If Beattie's not a mutie, then how can she see Red when Rory's in his man-self? *I* can't."

"I can't answer that. My minx can't either. Anything my minx can't answer is going to stay unanswered, on the whole." He rubbed his nose. "Our little miss sees true, though. What she said about Master Floppy in the barley straw was right enough."

"Warming his belly in the sun."

"Never you mind that, mistress. Let my minx tend to Master Floppy's belly." Abruptly, he got to his feet and held out a hand to Emer. "I'll say good-day to you now, Rory's queen. My minx might get ferocious if I spend too much time alone with any lovely maid but her or our blood."

Emer let him help her up, knowing that last was a joke . . . probably. Her visit was at an end, but she had no idea if it had been successful or not.

Jago Pendennis escorted her to the outskirts of Treborrow village, and then he paused to take her hand again. "I'll make you those rings, Rory's queen. Not all at once, mind, but when I have time to spare."

"What may I give you in return?"

His face creased in a grin. "Since you've found me out, I'll tell you. Any gift I choose to give to you and Rory is paid and repaid these several years. As you noted, my minx and I love Rory in our way, but there was only so much we could do for him.

"Annie Inkersoll left him in Berryman's charge, and Berryman gave him over to me for his mutie education. What none of us could do was give him true heart-love. He wouldn't have accepted it if we tried. That's why we're all of us grateful to you."

"It was nothing."

"It was a lot. There's not too many maids or misses or ladies who'd take on a child and be his friend and let him keep his secrets the way you did. There's even fewer who could be his love after that without doubting her own motives."

"Och, I had plenty o' doubts."

"But you overcame them—for him. You accepted his kissing ring."

Emer narrowed her eyes at him. "You knew I would want that. You charmed the thing. I couldn't wait to put it on, and I've never taken it off, except to shift it to my wedding finger. Nor will I take it off, until I go to glory."

And maybe not then.

Jago nodded. "My rings tend to stick to those who put them on. And it's true I charmed that kissing ring you wear. So did Emblyn. But no matter what charms we put into that metal, *no harm*. The spark of love had to be in you for them to *take*."

"So—"

"No more, Rory's queen. I don't care to talk about what I do or how I do it. Often, I don't know myself. I'll call on you, or Emblyn will, when I have rings for you."

"You could give them to Rory, or conjure them to the cottage."

"I could, but I won't. Make no mistake, mistress . . . this spark was born of *you*. Those rings need to be put into *your* hands and worn over *your* heart. Not for long, mind. Wear them for a spell, and then put them by somewhere safe and appropriate until they're needed."

Unexpectedly, he kissed her hand, and then, with a rueful smile, he blurred and dropped to become the spaniel.

Emer bent to pat him, careful not to touch the soft ears. Master Floppy made a playful pawing motion to touch her shoe, and then he turned and trotted off, tail wagging. He was heading for the St Botolph's gateway, she saw. He must be going *over there* to meet his minx and their granddaughter.

CHAPTER TWENTY-SIX: GINGER BEER

June 1957, *The Cottage, St Botolph's, and Shipley, Victoria*

More than a year after Emer struck her bargain with Jago Pendennis, Flower came back to the pixie forest.

Emer was startled when her sister arrived alone, riding on Fash, the kelpie, and with the pony, Glory-Be, trotting stoutly behind the mare.

"Flower!" She got up from her knees, where she'd been picking marigold flowers for a salve. She dumped the flowers into a basket and ran to meet her sister. On the way, she hurriedly conjured oatcakes for Fash and her companion.

Fash gave her a doubtful look and then a nudge. Glory-Be nickered sweetly, asking for a treat. Emer offered one in each hand, but her attention was on her sister.

"Flower — dearie, are Mam and Lambert all right?"

"They're fine, darlin' Emer. They'll come in a couple of months or so wid the fleet. They send you their dear love." Flower slid down from the kelpie's back and hugged Emer. "So, where are my nievies and the brother of my heart?"

"Rory's visiting parishioners *over there*, and the twins are somewhere or other."

"Ye've not lost me nievies, sister?"

"I have not. They've made friends with some of the treefolk children hereabouts. You know the tree maids take great care of their wee ones, so the twins are in safe hands."

Flower nodded gravely. "I remember. There are not many treefolk in Erin a' Fee or in the Star Pin. There are a few waterfolk . . . and seafolk of a kind at Dawn, I'm told, but not like the ones here."

Emer said, "What about yon mare and Glory-Be?"

"What about them?"

"I mean, what are they to do? You can't take them to Kerry's place *over there*."

"Sure, I didn't expect to. What did Fash do the time she carried Da to find Mam?"

Emer cast her mind back sixteen years.

Is it really so long?

"I don't know. I suppose she just . . ."

Ate up as much of the garden as she could.

Flower nodded. "Then, she can *just* do the same again. Not to worry, Emer." She gave Emer a second hug. "It's good to be back, though be sure I'll miss the green pastures of Erin a' Fee, an' the roses by the loch."

"And your gossoon?" Emer asked.

Flower looked away. "Him, always."

"Do you feel like telling me about him, dearie?"

"Not just now. I will, but—" She shrugged. "His name is Fionn Dearg . . . Fionn the Red, that is."

"I see." Emer remembered something. "Flower, you're fifteen now?"

"Sure and I am."

"Then you'll have chosen your last name? Or have you decided to keep O'Shea?"

Flower dropped her a curtsey. "I am Dervla Flower An Ghrá, at your service."

"But that's the name of the village on Bodhran Island. You've no' . . ." She broke off.

"I've not been there. I haven't enough years. Mam and Da have, though. That's where they planted me. I thought of Erin a' Fee, and of the brae house, here, and of your sweet cottage, and even of *Unicorn*, of the fair wind fleet, but it came to me those mark stages of me life. I thought of the darlin' quilt you and Mam made for me, but *Dervla Flower Quilt* seemed not such a good idea. I really began in a white cottage on that island. I was born there, too, did ye know?"

"I did not." Emer had always assumed Flower was born in the cottage at Rósanna Locha.

"Mam had a fancy to go back there with Da before being tied down to rearin' another child, but she *would* dance at the ceilidh and . . ." She spread her hands. "Sure, I was in a hurry an' I came squalling into Da's hands. Mam said niver was a gossoon so green as Da was when he found he was to be her midwife! So, Flower An Ghrá, I am and will be until I go to glory."

Emer understood that. Dornie had taken Lambert's name, as she had originally taken David Drumwiddy's, but Flower, for all her mixed blood, had thrown hard to *colleen*. Erin a' Fee was strong in her voice.

"Sure, ye're a little bit colleen, too," Flower pointed out when Emer suggested this.

"By blood, but no' by —" Emer broke off, indicating her full figure, which was definitely *brae*, although it came to her that since moving to the pixie forest, loving Rory, and knowing Hazel, brae was less present in her voice. "Rory will be home the bye, and I expect he'll fetch the twins along on his way. Come on in, and we'll have tea. Then, we'll see about taking you to Kerry . . . unless you want to wait for Mam and your da?"

"No, I'll go sooner. Otherwise, it will be hanging over me."

That seemed an odd thing to say, but Emer said, "Dearie, you'll have company. Beattie Hammett is going to Kerry at *Fayhaven* as well."

"But she can't be fifteen. Little bit of a thing, she was."

"She's not so small now — and sometimes folk go twice, though usually, the first time is before they begin to conjure. I think Beattie was waiting for you."

"*I* can conjure." Flower sounded surprised at herself. "I know colleens generally don't, but Da says that's more a matter o' custom than o' rule." She looked up. "Ah, here come the others. Best tell Rory to let Red be the one to meet wid Fash."

Flower expressed delight at the size and vigour of the twins, and pleasure at seeing Rory again. She declined Emer's offer of a bed and betook herself to the brae house for the night, but she was back next day and said she was ready to head out *over there* to Cousin Kerry's.

Emer perceived she was nervous, but there was nothing she could do about that. Flower would just have to learn the ways of *over there*.

Have to? And why?

As Lambert had once said, the nearest gateway to Erin a' Fee was a complex trip through the chain of islands called the Star Pin. Flower could *pass,* as the saying went, but if she wed a gossoon, as she seemed set to do, *he* never could, so of what benefit would knowledge of *over there* be to Flower?

Still, I always thought it would be of no use to me, either, but see me now — going to service with Rory, and visiting with Hazel. It's as well I don't run scared at the sound of a motor car, and I can even name some radio music if anyone asks.

If Flower changes her mind about that gossoon, she might want to live some of her life over there.

They could go through the pixie forest gate, but that would mean conjuring a message to Kerry and waiting in the copse for a good while. Emer generally stepped through a day before, conjured the message, and waited at home next day for Kerry to come to her. Kerry and her man lived closer to the St Botolph's gate, in any case. Emer recalled her bewilderment, as a young lassie, when Kerry tried to explain what she called *the tyranny of distance* to her untutored cousin. Emer still didn't quite accept it. *Over here,* one just *went* to familiar places. The reason one couldn't just *go* to visit Dornie at Erin a' Fee, so she understood, was because there was so much featureless country in between that no one could hold the necessary knowledge of the route.

Fash knew, no doubt, but Fash wasn't telling, and besides, she lived at Erin a' Fee. It seemed that the same situation applied to travel *over there*, except that it extended to brief journeys over known routes. Folk *over there* wasted a deal of time in moving from one place to another. That was why they used motor cars and buses and — Emer shivered — aeroplanes.

Accordingly, Emer and Rory took Flower and the twins to Berryman and Clover Grene at the manse. They left the twins there with Melody Peckerdale. Melody was Peter Peckerdale's daughter, an enchanting black-haired pixie miss somewhat older than the twins. Emer didn't know Peter well, but she remembered he had dashed in while Berryman was blessing Emer and Rory at their wedding.

Melody said she was happy to play with the twins under Great-Granny Clover's supervision. She explained, in her articulate way, that her baby brother Kristos was as yet too young to *play properly*. She would love to draw pictures and seek beetles with Davey and Andorie.

Having got the twins settled, Emer and Rory borrowed Dorcas and the cart and drove Flower and her baggage, which she'd conjured from home, along to the gateway.

Rory looped the reins on Dorcas's neck and gave her an apple, conjured from the winter store in the gateway stables. Then he tapped her shoulder and sent her home to the manse. He took Emer's hand and Flower's, and they stepped through the gateway and walked the short distance to the churchyard.

They expected to send a message to Kerry, but it proved unnecessary, as Hazel Charming was just getting into her car, a large vehicle she called a *station wagon*. She saw the Inkersolls and Flower and got out again.

"My dear Emer . . . and Rory. And . . ."

"My wee sister, Flower," Emer reminded her.

"Of course. Not so *wee* now! Are you going to stay with Missus Palmer, Flower? Beattie Hammett is there, and my Nancy is pouting because she can't stay, too. I've tried to explain to her that she doesn't *need* to learn to *pass* since she *lives human*. She can learn what she needs from me, but she still thinks it most unfair."

"Nancy Charming is a halfling," Emer reminded Flower, who was looking perplexed.

"Then should she not be sponsored in the forest?" Flower asked.

"That would seem fair, but Nancy often goes with her grandparents, when they go up to the chalk cliffs. She spends a good deal of the school holidays there with her sisters. She wanted Beattie to come to us, but Beattie needs schooling, which I can't provide."

Emer recalled the holiday home Kerry Palmer ran with her man in a beach-side township called Shipley. In the summer, the rooms of *Fayhaven* were filled with children from the city, but in what Kerry called *the off season,* she took in young fay and patiently taught them the use of the telephone, of electric stoves, how to catch a bus, how to use money, and even, for the older ones, how to drive a car.

Her man, Ian Palmer, was a teacher, so the small school, where some human children came for extra tutoring, could easily be adapted for visiting fay.

Emer realised Hazel had asked her a question.

She fumbled for an answer, but her friend simply laughed. "Oh, Emer, you were off with the fairies! And what a very odd term that is, in the circumstances. You weren't having an attack of *the sight,* were you?"

"No, just recalling my own time with Kerry. That was in nineteen thirty-six . . . such a long time ago."

"I remember you saying you'd not been *over here* in years

until you began coming with Rory. *Fayhaven* is a little changed since then, I suspect."

"Aye, it has grown some."

"And the school is a bit more official. Did you know Ian has two more teachers working with him this year?"

"I don't think so."

"Well, not to worry. Is Kerry coming to collect you today, or would you like me to drive you down to Shipley? It's no trouble."

Over the year and a half of their friendship, Emer had learned that nothing seemed to be any trouble to Hazel.

"That would be lovely, if you can spare the time," she said.

Rory glanced over at the church. It was a fleeting look, but Emer recognised it. "If you'd like to go into the church for a wee while, Flower and I can go with Hazel, and I'll meet you back at the cottage," she said.

Rory gave her his dazzling smile and kissed her. "Thank you, my queen." He kissed Flower on the brow. "Goodbye for now, *deirfiúr mo chroí*, I'll see you again soon." He turned and went across the sward to the church door.

Emer realised Hazel was looking at her with curiosity. "He called her *sister of my heart*," she said, smiling.

"I see . . . but it wasn't that. Has Rory got some business in the church? I've just finished taking out the dead flowers. Missus Raintree usually does it, but she's got her daughter in hospital with her third baby."

Emer was glad not to have encountered Missus Raintree, who always made her nervous. She smiled. "Och, no . . . Rory just likes to spend a wee while in there in what he calls *silent communion*." She added, "Not that he often gets the chance. He's almost always with someone . . . family or flock."

"I see," Hazel said again. She indicated the station wagon. "Flower, you can get in the back seat. Have you been in a car before?"

Flower shook her head.

"It's rather like a cart or a wagon, but it goes faster and makes more noise. Do you need Emer to sit beside you?"

"No — sure and I'll be fine."

"Very good. If you need to stop on the way, let me know."

Emer opened the door for her sister and watched her settle herself. "It's no' so very far," she said, although it was certainly farther than *she* liked. That was why Kerry visited her rather than the other way around. She climbed in beside Hazel and waited, with a lurch of fear, for the roar of the engine. She wrinkled her nose at the smell of petrol, which she heartily disliked. It had to be endured, so she tried to converse normally as if her heart wasn't hammering.

"Relax, Emer. All that tensing up is bad for your blood pressure. Well, it would be if you were human," Hazel said.

They drove down to the coast and around loops of small bays until they reached the town of Shipley. Emer remembered it as being much smaller during her visits there as a young lassie, and she wondered how it seemed to Flower, who had never been anywhere larger than a village.

"There's the lighthouse," she said, half to herself.

"Shipley Light. Yes, that was built back in the eighteen forties," Hazel said. She slowed the car. "Flower, do you want to have a look at the lighthouse? There's a nice view from the top, and you might solve the secret of the steps. It's said no one has ever made an accurate count of them."

Flower said nothing. Emer realised she'd barely spoken during the journey. She mentally scolded herself for being too caught up in conversation with Hazel to notice.

She turned to look and saw her sister's usually rosy complexion was pale and almost green. "What's the matter, hen?" she asked with concern.

Flower simply stared at her with pained eyes.

"What is it?" Hazel stopped the car and looked over her

shoulder. "Oh dear . . . do you feel sick, Flower?"

Flower said nothing.

"Emer? Oh, you folk hardly know what that means. I know Matt doesn't, and the girls are practically immune to all the childhood diseases." She focused on Flower again. "Do you have a bad feeling inside you, my dear?"

After a moment, Flower nodded.

"Motion sickness. Are you a bad sailor? I mean, do you feel sick in boats?"

"She was fine when she came to the forest off *Unicorn*," Emer said. Then she remembered Flower had arrived this last time on the kelpie mare. "Flower, did you feel bad on your way back to Erin a' Fee?"

Flower closed her eyes and gave an infinitesimal nod.

"I think the best thing we can do is to get her into the fresh air," Hazel said. She got out and opened the door for Flower. "Come on, sweetie. It's not too far from here. I think you and Emer might want to walk. I'll take your stuff to *Fayhaven* and let Kerry know you'll be along soon."

Emer perceived she and Flower were being organised, but Hazel was right. It seemed the best thing.

She put her arm around her suffering sister.

"I wish I had the loving touch, dearie. I don't expect your touch works on yoursel'?"

"No," Flower murmured.

Hazel said, "I'll just pop over to the shop and get you some ginger beer. That should help." Without waiting for an answer, she hurried across the street, with her wide green skirts swinging.

Emer gazed after her.

I remember this. The sight *showed me the lighthouse and a human woman in bright skirts. That was Hazel before I knew her!*

She led Flower to a wooden seat under a tree. "Sit down, dearie."

Flower did so. Her cheeks gradually lost their green tinge.

She said, "Mistress Charming is a very managing lady."

"Aye, and a kind one. You ken fine ginger is good for the insides."

Soon, Hazel was back with a stoneware bottle. She removed the lid and said to Emer, "Wait a bit until it goes flat. Then, when your sister's feeling more the thing, you can bring her to Kerry's. Do you remember the way? If not, I can leave the car and walk with you."

"I know it."

"Or I can have Ian bring the dray?"

"No, we'll walk," Emer said.

"Do you need coats? It's a bit cold."

Emer thought about coats, which had sleeves and which restricted her movements. She considered them one of the nastier of human-style garments. She pulled her shawl more tightly around her and conjured one out of Flower's baggage for her sister. "See, Hazel? We're fine with good braeside wool."

An hour later, Flower was feeling very much better, and they were well on their way to *Fayhaven*, cheeks stinging in the bracing winter wind.

"It's a bonnie place, and you'll be happy here. Kerry and her man will look after you, and you'll know Beattie and maybe some others," Emer said.

"And ye'll be visitin' me?"

"Of course, and so will Mam and Lambert when they come."

"Sure, that's grand to hear, because after that *motor car*, I doubt I'll be visiting *you*," Flower said.

Emer sighed. She'd just realised that Lambert, as a green gossoon, would have considerable trouble visiting Shipley. Folk—human folk—would stare.

Chapter Twenty-Seven: Five Whole Years

December 1957, *The Cottage*

Emer's thirty-fifth birthday and Rory's twenty-third coincided with the fifth anniversary of their wedding.

Dornie and Lambert were soon heading back home on the fair winds fleet. They wanted to spend the last few days with their daughter, so they had gone to Shipley to retrieve Flower. She was still at Kerry's, and the difficulty of getting her back had loomed large until two days before when Peter Peckerdale came up with a possible solution.

He'd learned of the problem when he'd brought his daughter, Melody, and his small son, Kristos, to visit their great-grandparents at the manse. He'd stormed into the parlour and stated his miss needed to rest and he intended to rest with her. Therefore, he informed his grandparents that they had the privilege of spending time with their great-grandchildren.

Finding Dornie, Emer and Lambert there already, he'd decided to drink tea with them before departing to rest with his miss. They all knew, and Peter Peckerdale probably knew they knew, just what kind of rest Peter had in mind.

As she and Rory enjoyed that kind of rest, too, Emer attached no blame to him.

Bairns will be off into the world in their own good time. A man and his wife should not be strangers to one another when that happens.

Emer and Rory had got to enjoy their rests rather often

since Dornie and Lambert's return, as Dornie doted upon her grandchildren and Lambert, like all leprechaun men, had a powerful sense of family, whether by blood or by love. Emer was sorry they were leaving, but she and Rory had decided to visit Erin a' Fee in a year or so with the twins.

Peter's personality tended to overwhelm any room he entered, but Emer barely flinched when he said abruptly to Dornie, "Your miss still *over there*, then, Mistress O'Shea?"

"Indade," Lambert said, answering for them both.

"Not getting into trouble?"

Dornie stared at him, lips parted in puzzlement. Clearly, she found Peter rather too much of a challenge. Most people did.

"Well, *I* got into trouble," Peter said. He frowned. "Got in a proper pickle. Had a miss who didn't want to be my miss, made a fucking old gaylord friend who died on me—posed in my skin for a swan picture. Had to *loom*. Came back with soul cold." He shrugged. "Then I fell over my miss in the forest, and it was all right after that. It was fucking wonderful! Still is."

"Language, Peter," Clover Grene said.

"Sorry, Grandma. Wonderful, except this dratted priest made us wait to be wedded." His sideways glance left no one in any doubt of which dratted priest he meant.

"Peter, that's enough," his grandmother said in a soft but decided voice.

"I'm sure Flower's not getting into that kind of trouble," Emer said into the silence.

"No?"

"No. But she does have a wee problem."

Peter Peckerdale turned his extraordinary turquoise eyes on her. "What is it? My father-by-love's a bloody fix-it pixie. Might help."

Emer felt, oddly, that he really wanted to know. She said,

"Master Peckerdale, you know how to drive a motor car, do you not?"

"Not only drive one. *Got* one. Take my miss out in it *over there*. Go to see our friends, and use it when Magda gets me some work. So?"

Emer had no idea who *Magda* was, but she said, "I see. I've been in motor cars sometimes. I don't like them, though I do manage. But when my friend Hazel drove Flower to our cousin *over there*, Flower felt so bad she won't get back in a motor car."

"Scared," Peter diagnosed. "Stands to reason. She's a colleen, right? Probably doesn't get *over there* much. Poor maid."

"Not scared. Hazel said it was motion sickness. Have you ever had that?"

He shook his head. "Heard of it though, from Tommy. Fucking horrible. She'd better stay out of cars. And fucking buses. Those are worse, Tommy says. Tommy has to drive himself because he feels all wrong if someone else does it."

Emer didn't know who Tommy was, either, but she persisted. "She's at Shipley, which is a long way from the gates. Too far to walk *over there*."

He nodded his comprehension. "So you want a way to get her back this side."

"Aye, that's it. We thought of a dray, but the roads are so busy . . . Still, it might come to that."

Peter frowned. He seemed to do that a lot, but Emer thought he was genuinely trying to help. Then he said, "You got that kelpie, right? Fecking nasty thing tried to bite me when I came to talk to your man about getting our Kris baptised."

Emer considered Fash, who had, at different times, carried her, Lambert, Dornie and Flower long distances with little complaint. She could indeed be *fecking nasty* if she *took against* someone.

"I remember. She tries to bite Rory, too, though she likes Red. What about her?"

"Get it to carry your miss back to the gateway."

"But—"

His frown deepened. "Tell you what, I'll get Tommy to borrow us a horsebox. Anything Tommy can't borrow can't be borrowed. Fucking marvellous what he can do. Bring it to the pixie forest gate and get the fucking kelpie inside. Drive to this Shipley place, decant the kelpie and have your young colleen get on her back." He looked pleased with himself. "Nothing stops a kelpie going where it wants to be . . . right? Bad as bogles. And that kelpie will want to be this side of the gate. I fucking well guarantee that kelpie will *not* want to be *over there*. She'll have your colleen back at the pixie forest gate in two shakes of a tail."

So it was going to be that easy? Emer couldn't believe Lambert and Dornie would consider this mad scheme, but they did.

"I still have the kelpie bottle you gave to me," she reminded Lambert.

He said, "That's for *you*, darlin' Emer, not for a little bit of a problem like this one."

Emer thought he might not think it such a little bit of a problem if he'd seen Flower's pallor, but then she recalled he must have seen her when she felt *travel sickness,* as Hazel called it, on the galleon.

Sighing, she left Flower's welfare to her parents.

The dear knows when I'll use that bottle . . .

Now, two days after Peter Peckerdale's extraordinary notion, Lambert and Dornie had gone to Shipley with Peter, his miss, Pia, their human friends, Judit and Tommy, and various children, including the twins.

"How *did* we let them take the twins?" Emer lamented to Rory an hour after the party left.

They were getting ready to attend the church fete. It wasn't the way Emer wanted to spend their birthdays and wedding anniversary, but it was her duty to go. The fete was being organised by various ladies of the congregation, and since Berryman Grene had handed over almost all the parish duties to Rory, they had to be present.

Rory put his arms around her. "Mistress Inkersoll, you look magnificent in that gown. The colour is most becoming."

"Dinna change the subject."

"They'll be all right. I think Lambert is depending on Flower not wanting to lose face before her nievies."

"But what if—"

He stopped her with a kiss. "What's wrong, my darling? It's not like you to fret over the twins. They always land on their feet."

"Aye, and butter side up." She thought about her much-loved son and daughter. At just over four years old, Davey and Andorie had developed formidable personalities. They had their father's charm, and Emer hoped they also had his innate goodness. It was difficult to tell. Davey would talk to anyone. Andorie had less to say, but whatever she did say was her final word on a subject. Parting them so they could spend time for separate activities had proved impossible. Andorie liked to draw, while Davey favoured beetle-watching. They preferred doing each of these things together to doing their preferred things apart.

Rory kissed his way along her jaw and down her neck. Dornie had surprised her that morning with a new gown of such light lavender-coloured stuff Emer felt she might as well wear her petticoat. Rory insisted it was the most becoming thing he'd ever seen.

Emer felt the familiar stirring of desire. "Rory . . ."

He fondled her breast.

"We have to go—"

"No, my love, we *have* to do this." He conjured off the clothing they had just put on and sat down on the edge of their bed, bringing her to stand between his knees. "You see the state of me? Hardly fitting for a church fete."

Emer laughed. She climbed into his lap, straddling him and bringing his face against her breasts. "I can hardly believe we've been wed for five whole years. Do you remember our first time in bed together?" she said in his ear.

He stopped kissing her to say, "Lord, yes!" He raised laughing amber eyes to her face. "I was so keyed up I couldn't think. I didn't want to disappoint you."

"You feel keyed up right now," she observed.

"Oh, I am."

"And you have never disappointed me. Not ever. You never will."

He got to his feet, supporting her thighs with his strong hands. Then he turned suddenly and deposited her on the bed, coming down on top of her. "Mistress Inkersoll, are you going to move?"

She giggled. "Darling Rory, how can I? I have a husband on top of me."

Emer wanted to stay in bed and enjoy the dreamy post-loving interlude to the full, but after a few minutes of lazy kissing and stroking, Rory sighed. "We'd better go, my queen. Otherwise, your friend, Hazel, might prevail on Matt to let her through the gate so she can come and fetch us."

"She might, too!" Emer sat up. "I wish I had time for a tub."

Rory conjured her a warm washcloth instead.

"I wish we had time to—" Emer broke off. She had made a private vow *never* to suggest, by word or by manner, that the duties of Rory's calling could be irksome to her.

"We have plenty of time," Rory said, putting his arms around her.

"Aye, we do." Emer put more brae into her voice, for it always made him smile. "I was being a wee bitty selfish. Ye ken fine, I'm as proud as proud of my ain fine priest and his role in bringing folk to the Lord."

"I don't bring them to the Lord, my queen. That's a thing folk have to do for themselves."

"Aye, but when they see how *you* are, they just naturally want to walk the path with you." She saw him looking serious and said, "Now let us go to this fete before Hazel comes after us. You'll do yon duty, and I'll do mine, and then we can come back here and get into bed and stay there until we feel like getting out . . ."

"Or until our twins come home," Rory said. He added, "Oh, I almost forgot. Did Mistress Clover tell you about needing spending money at the fete?"

"She did."

"I have some here for you. You know how —"

"I ken fine how to spend coins. Kerry taught me back in the day."

The thought of Kerry brought Flower back into her mind.

Oh dear, I hope this mad scheme of Master Peckerdale's works out.

CHAPTER TWENTY-EIGHT: FETE OR FATE

December 1957, *St Botolph's*

Emer and Rory were a little late for the St Botolph's Church Fete, and when they arrived, Hazel Charming was directing things admirably. When she saw Emer, she hugged her, wished her a happy birthday and a happy anniversary, admired her new gown and said, all being well, she would now slip away and leave Emer to take over.

Emer took this for Hazel's tacit assurance that *she*, Mistress Emer Inkersoll, was the lady of St Botolph's and had no need to be managed by the bishop's wife.

"I think there's no' too much to do now," she said, laughing.

"Well, there wasn't much to do in the first place. Everyone knows the drill," Hazel assured her. She waved her arm at the stalls set up in the church grounds. "I understand most churches depend heavily on their parishioners for donations and funds, but dear St Botolph's is not the same."

"No, there's nobbut t' pay t' parson," Emer said, mimicking Matt Charming's hob accent to make his wife laugh.

"Nor for maintenance and repairs. It took me a long time to understand that, but Matt finally got it through my head that the fay churches, few as they are, are some of the best maintained and attended in the country. Of course, it helps when good folk like the Bless family can organise repairs and inspections that cost nothing but labour. Do you know them?"

Emer shook her head. "Rory's mentioned there were

builders who *live human*, but I don't think we've met. It sounds like an alpenfee name."

"It is. Jan Bless and his brother, Klein. Nice men. They drink like fish, out of ridiculously big steins, but of course, that never affects them — much."

Emer was surprised it affected them at all! "I suppose they must have leprechaun poteen in those steins," she said.

"Oh?"

"That's the only thing that affects most fay, and that, only some of us."

"You?"

"I have no idea. Lambert brews it at home in Rósanna Locha, but he never offered me any when I was there. He said he was unsure how it might affect a braefolk lassie with a touch of the green way in her blood, but I think he knows very well, since Mam is just that. I have no doubt he shares a dram or two with her."

Hazel laughed. "I thought leprechauns didn't lie?"

"They don't, but they can be what Mam calls *economical wid the truth.*"

"How lucky I am to be married to a darling uncomplicated hob man then! I'll leave you to do the rounds in your own time, Emer. I know your folk don't use money, but some of the human stall folk do . . ."

"Och, Mistress Grene told me about that. Though Master Berryman never needed paying, there *is* provision made for what he calls *appropriate use.* He handed that provision on to Rory when he stepped back, and Rory gave me some to use today."

"I should have known that. I hope you didn't think I was being —"

Emer put down the basket of scones she'd brought as a contribution to the fete, put her arms around Hazel and hugged her. "Dearie, you are *not* interfering. I couldna wish for a kinder friend."

Hazel kissed her cheek. "Mm, your special scones! I might have to buy those myself. Emer, I know I'm sometimes bossy, so I'm glad you don't mind. Now, where's young Davey? Has he gone off to find Matt and talk about cheese? Matt's got hold of some Teesdale cheese, made from ewes' milk, would you believe? Apparently, the French Cistercian monks had something to do with it . . ."

"Och, Davey will be sorry to miss that. He and Andorie are away with Mam and Lambert," Emer said. She didn't go into the whole tale of Flower and the kelpie and Peter Peckerdale's scheme, because that was just bizarre. Besides, it would take all day. She resolved to tell it to Hazel when the matter was resolved.

Hazel went off to find her girls, and Emer began her careful way around the stalls, pausing to speak to the parishioners. She was careful to buy or to trade something at each one.

By now she'd got to know most of the regular visitors to the church, and although some of them probably missed the capable wisdom Clover Grene had been wont to dispense, the congregation had taken the new reverend's wife to their hearts. Emer knew the names of their children and prepared herself to share in any news they wanted to discuss. The church and its environs were charmed and warded, so the place was joyous and welcoming. No wonder Rory loved it.

The fete added bright colours to the dreaming stones, and the air was full of the scent of flowers, fruit and baked goods. Emer thought of her mother and Flower and wished they were there.

Och, there are plenty of festivals in Erin a' Free . . . and fewer humans to complicate matters.

She had gone around almost all of the stalls when she caught sight of one under the oak tree where her mother and father-by-love had been kissing when she first met Hazel.

At first, it appeared to be untenanted. Then she perceived

the top of a red head showing above the carved wooden wares.

Rory? She hurried over and paused uncertainly as a lean, long-fingered hand suddenly reached up from behind the stall. It held a wooden whistle that looked remarkably like the one Emblyn Pendennis had lent her to call in Master Floppy when she visited Treborrow to ask about rings.

The hand was like Rory's, but could not be his. For one thing, it lacked the beloved copper ring, set with ambers and mother-of-pearl. He would never take it off . . . until . . .

No . . . Lord save me . . .

Emer reeled as *the sight* hit her.

Rory.

It was Rory grown older by far, with his hair part-grey and his hand holding hers. They lay together on their bed, and she had her head on his shoulder.

He said, *Love you, darling. See you soon,* and he kissed her brow.

Shaken, Emer stared into the vision. *But that's what we're to say if we ever spend a night apart. How can that be? Is one of us going away? No' to see Mam . . . she'll be gone to glory. Flower?*

Her frantic thoughts faded as she heard his dear voice again, back across the years . . .

Darling Emer. Would you like to have my ring to wear? Or should I have yours?

Emer – Emer – oh, my queen!

The grief in his voice brought her to tears.

No, no, no . . .

Someone put a hand on her shoulder, and she blinked, aware tears were streaming down her cheeks. She saw a blur of red hair and pale skin, but it wasn't her Rory, now, then or ever. It was a stranger who smelled of freshly planed wood.

She froze, caught in horror and embarrassment as a concerned gaze met hers.

"Missus . . . *Mistress* Inkersoll? What's wrong? Can I do

anything to help?"

She tried to pull herself together. "It's all right. Just a touch of *the sight.*"

"As much an affliction as a comfort, I take it," he said dryly.

"Sometimes." She sniffled, realising he wasn't quite a stranger after all. "Mister Folly. You served me with tea at my husband's ordination."

"So I did. And got a right bollocking from Vera Raintree for paying you too much attention. I think she suspected my intentions."

"Och, I think she was more concerned with getting her own tea. I was holding up the queue."

"Could be." He flicked his hand and gave her a white handkerchief, soft and old, and laundered with lavender.

She had dabbed away the tears and composed herself before she realised the significance of this and made a sound of surprise.

He raised an eyebrow. "Never say my red hair's disconcerting you *now*? Your husband and son are similarly blessed, I know." He gestured to where Rory stood laughing with a young couple who must be consulting him about a baptism. The woman was heavy with child.

"It's no' the hair."

"What then?"

"Och, it's just that I thought you were human, Master Folly. Then, you conjured just now."

"I *am* mostly human. Mum's purely human and my father is, or was, a halfling, or so I believe. Have you ever met Mum? I know she was there when I served you that tea."

Emer remembered the upright old lady who had been talking to Clover Grene.

"I did not care to interrupt her tea. And I don't think I've seen either of you since the ordination."

"I've been to a couple of services, but you've not been

there. No!" He raised his long hand. "That's not criticism. You always support Father Rory, just by being his wife and the mother of his children. You have no need to come to every service."

Emer looked down at the handkerchief.

This must be his mother's. "That's what Rory says."

"He's right."

"Is your mother here today?"

A shadow passed over his face.

"I hope nothing's wrong."

"Not a thing, but she doesn't get about now. I thought I might ask Father Rory to visit her again, because the doctor says she hasn't long. She's not ill, just very old."

"I see. I'm sorry."

He said, "So am I. Mum's been the one constant in my life. She's asked me to make her coffin. She insists on having it for inspection before she goes."

Emer blinked.

He laughed. "I suppose it's logical enough, since I work with wood." He indicated the wares on the stall.

Emer looked down at them. "These are lovely," she said, eyeing the boxes and miniature cabinets. She ran her fingers over the lid of a round box with drawers in the sides. The brass hasp was in perfect scale. It reminded her of something.

The box I saw that time with the sight. *The one that held the rings.*

Jago Pendennis had been giving her rings for months now. She kept them, prosaically, in a drawstring bag Dornie had made for her, but they needed something bigger . . . *more appropriate.*

I should buy one of these boxes to hold them.

She knew she wouldn't. The box *the sight* had shown her wasn't on the stall. These were smaller.

"John, do you make things to order?"

"Apart from Mum's coffin?"

She smiled at the rather grim joke. "Aye."

"Well, I make these whistles in *found wood* that folk bring to me. Some of them like a keepsake from a fallen tree they've loved."

"I think I've seen one of your whistles before . . . but I need a ring box."

"Take your pick." He indicated a dozen or so, carved in different woods, inlaid and polished to a deep, soft gleam.

"Not those wee ones, lovely though they are. I need a big one, to hold a great many rings." She told him about her project. Then, after a little thought, she told him of what *the sight* had shown her. "Only I had no idea where I'd get the box until I saw your work here."

"That sounds interesting. You can describe it to me, or draw it."

"I'm no hand at drawing. Rory might."

"Father Rory draws?"

"Aye, he's good at a great many things," she said with pride. She hurried on, "It should be about *so* big." She held her hands apart to show. "It should have a brass hasp, and I'd like it carved with sprigs of heather and crosses."

"I suppose the heather is for the brae and the crosses for your husband's calling," he said, nodding.

"Aye, and there were flowers, so. Catsears."

He looked at her thoughtfully. "*Catsears?*"

"Like a wee dandelion, with longer stems, branching . . . you ken?"

"I'm sure I can find some to study. But *why?*"

It occurred to Emer that John Folly, as a quarterling and an occasional parishioner, might not know about Red. Mutable fay were common, especially among courtfolk and in the brae, but the extreme mutability Rory and Jago Pendennis displayed was rare even *over there*. She couldn't see how a mutie of that order could live full-time in the human realm.

She said, "It's what I saw with *the sight,* and it has a meaning for my Rory and me."

"I'll do my best," John said. He smiled at her. "It will be something cheerful to engage my mind when I need a respite from working on Mum's coffin."

"Does she have a great many instructions for that?" Emer asked.

"She has indeed. She wants heather on it, too, and she wants a nameplate to match her husband's." He grimaced. "That is going to be difficult, since he passed on in eighteen eighty-five, and I was not present at the time."

"*What?*" Emer spoke without thinking.

"Well, yes. He passed in these parts and is buried in the graveyard over yonder. Mum had him put in a double plot, being a thrifty Scot. She thought it would save paying out extra when her time came. She's described the nameplate, but after seventy-odd years how well does she remember?"

"Young man! Are you going to serve us or not?"

Emer turned at the pre-emptory voice. Without surprise, she saw Vera Raintree and three of her friends, all wearing interesting hats. She smiled at them. "Ladies. There are some lovely wee boxes here for your rings and trinkets, and some wooden whistles you may want for playing, but I must away to my husband." She added, to John, "I'll tell Rory your mother would like fine to see him. Never fear, he won't pray over her unless she would like it."

"I'm sure she'll be happy to see him again." He looked about to say more, but a hat wonderfully decorated with cherries bobbed menacingly, so he turned to discuss trinket boxes with his customers.

Chapter Twenty-nine: Lavender

December 1957, *St Botolph's*

Emer thought she should make good on her words, so she went to where Rory, who had finished with the parents-to-be, was consuming cream cake with two tall, fair-haired alpenfee men. The Bless brothers, she assumed, and she was proved correct when Rory introduced her. He said he'd been arranging a musical evening for the week before Christmas, and Jan and Klein had promised to bring their hackbretts along.

The men offered Emer a plate of cream cake.

When she praised the delicious stuff, Jan said it was called *alpenkuchen*.

"It's made from my own recipe." He sounded smug.

"It's wonderful!"

Emer hoped it had no leprechaun poteen in it. If it had, and if they'd been sharing it with humans, the dear Lord knew what effect it might have.

This interlude so distracted Emer that it wasn't until the fete was winding down that she remembered to tell Rory about Elsie Folly's decline.

"She's no' ill, John says. Maybe it's *the slip*."

"I don't think that affects humans," Rory said doubtfully. "But of course I'll go to her in a day or so. She may have some final strictures for me," he added.

"Not today?"

"Someone else has the right to my undivided attention

today."

"Her son is making her casket," Emer said.

"That's a kind thought."

"Och, she asked him to do it."

"That's what I meant. It was a kind thought of the old lady's. It lets him do her a last service."

Emer hadn't looked at it that way. Had John?

Rory looked around at the diminishing crowd. "My queen, do you think we might properly take our leave?"

"I do."

Hand in hand, they stepped through the St Botolph's gateway and headed home to the cottage. Rory stopped Emer at the gateway and kissed her. "You look like lavender come to life in that gown."

"Lavender *is* alive, you daft laddie."

"You know what I mean."

"I do. Rory."

"Yes?"

He looked up, with the slanting sunlight lighting his amber eyes and red hair.

"I had another bout of *the sight* today."

He went on gazing at her, waiting.

"I've been wondering whether to tell you what I saw."

"Is there a reason not to?"

"I'm no' so sure," she said, troubled. She took his hand and brought their ring-fingers together. "It's to do with our rings."

"Maybe you should tell me, then. Did you want another one . . . a new one to be your wedding band?"

"*This* dear ring is my everything-band." She sat down on a loveseat she'd put in the lavender and drew him to sit with her. "I saw us a long way ahead. I was — very old."

He looked at her steadily.

"We were still wearing these rings, and you asked me if you should wear mine, or if I might wear yours."

"Swap them, do you mean?" He bent his head to examine the rings, although he must be as familiar with them as she was.

"I think you meant one of us might wear them both when I go to glory."

He said nothing, so she prompted gently, "Is that what you'd like?"

"I never thought of that."

"Nor did I, but you *will* think of it — then — and it might be nice to find an answer now so we'll both be serene in our minds when the time comes."

She thought he might protest, but he asked, "What would you like to have happen?"

Never leave you and wear your ring forever.

That was impossible, so she said, "I thought Andorie might like to have my ring, but then, we might have another lassie."

A lassie we'll call Amber.

She continued, "So, I think it would be more fitting if Andorie has one of her own while she can enjoy it without sorrow. We might get Master Pendennis to make her one. It would be too big at present, but she could wear it around her neck on a chain until she's grown."

"What about a bracelet? That could be made with a tuck in it to let out as she grows," Rory suggested.

"Aye. That's better. That's perfect. Then she can have a ring from her love the way I did, and a bracelet will do as well for her as bairn and lady. And we can get something for Davey."

He smiled. "Not a bracelet. I can't see our son wearing one, although pisky men and leppies do."

"Nor can I, but I'd like him to have a keepsake from us both while we've many years left to see him enjoy it."

Rory said, "I wonder would he like a silver whistle?"

Emer thought of the wooden whistles John made, but she knew Davey's gift should match Andorie's in material.

"Could Master Jago make that?" she asked.

"I believe the old dog would enjoy the challenge."

"Then that's the thing for the laddie. It can have a chain to go around his neck."

Rory said, "Mum had a wooden whistle. I think it might have been made of oak wood. She played it sometimes. It was wonderfully sweet-toned."

"Oh?"

"When she went to glory, Berry asked if I would like to have it, but I wanted her to keep it, so we put it on a chain around her neck, and tucked it in her favourite gown. I think I had a fancy I might still hear her playing if it went to rest with her."

"Did you ever?"

"No-oo . . ."

Emer looked at him steadily.

He said, "Do you remember when we met?"

"Aye. You were naked on my floor and invoking the holy mother."

"Not that. When you met Red."

"Of course! He swung on my skirts, poor wee mannie."

"I don't think I ever told you how he — I — came to be there, then, to meet you."

Emer felt a stab of conscience. "Oh dear, and I never thought to ask."

"You *always* let me keep my own thoughts, my darling queen," he said as he'd said before.

"Aye . . . so how did wee Red come to be out in the forest that day?"

"We were listening for the music . . . and we heard it. I did, I mean. I doubt if Red knows much about music. I followed it into the forest. It turned out to be a sweetwood flute, played by a sylvan, not by my mother. He was called Asht . . . Mum knew him slightly."

Emer nodded, identifying the sylvan in question. He lived

in the pixie forest with his forever and a tiny replica of themselves, whose name was Oash. Sylvan aged slowly and lived a long time, so they seldom made close friends with others in the pixie forest. They were nice folk, so extremely mutable they might be male or female, just as they felt at the time.

"So, Asht played the flute for you."

"He never even saw me. He was just playing, the way they do . . . but it was a tune Mum used to play to me. I don't know the name."

Emer's heart ached again for the bereft child she'd met so many years ago.

"I let Red take over without meaning to. That used to happen sometimes. *He* wasn't going to cry about the music. And then we saw you, and the sadness left forever," Rory said.

"Not quite forever."

He grimaced. "I've learned to forgive myself for that lapse in faith. *Would* you have taken off your kissing ring and never seen me again?"

Emer said, steadily, "Aye. It would have broken my heart to do it, but the alternative would have brought us both to ruin."

"But you didn't."

"I did not."

"Because I *considered prayerfully* and came back to you."

"Aye." She squeezed his hands and said, "But that's in the past. It brings us back to our rings and their future. I think I know what I'd be wishful for, but you'll be the one who'll have to live on with the decision, so it should be your choice."

He said, "I think we should each keep wearing our own. That's if—"

"That's what I thought, too." She kissed his hands in turn and blew out her cheeks in a whoosh of relief. "So, it's decided, and you'll no' need to ask that question and fret if I cannae answer."

And I will not be able to answer. I'll have gone too far to speak.

"Is that what you saw? Me fretting?"

"I cannot be sure. It was one interpretation. But now, you'll *know*. You can tell me something at the last, maybe, and not have to ask anything. I'll sleep well with my ambers watching over me, and you'll know the mother-of-pearl is still lighting your days."

He nodded and then grasped at the matter that must be important to him. "You say we were *old* when you saw us."

"I was very old, and you, not so much . . . but then, we knew that might happen. You'll live a grand long life, Master Inkersoll, and you'll have love, always."

"But we have a great many years together."

"That we have. No' more than the stars in the sky, but *many*."

He got to his feet and lifted Emer to hers.

"Are we going to bed?" she asked.

"Not as such. I'm about to cast a glamour, because I have ambitions to lie with you here, in the lavender, with the sunshine."

In the open air? In daylight? But what if —

Emer dismissed such thoughts. They had a lot of years ahead, and she meant to enjoy as many delights for as long as she possibly could.

Chapter Thirty: Borrowed Sunshine

February 1959, *Hazel's house, Over There*

It was a late summer's day when Emer finally laid eyes on the ring box she'd first seen in a vision three years before.

Elsie Folly had passed on a few weeks after the fete. She had requested a private funeral, *just my John and Father Rory to see me off*, as she'd put it, and John had not been to any services since.

One day, in Hazel's sitting room, Emer asked about him, in a roundabout way.

Hazel gave her a sharp, not unkindly, look and said, "I can't help you there, Emer. The cottage is rented out to Vera Raintree's son on a long lease, so I don't expect Little John means to come back for a good while, if ever."

"I see."

"I know Rory visited Elsie before she passed. If Little John said anything to him about his plans, maybe he knows more."

"If so, he has no' repeated it."

"And I assume Elsie took her secrets — and John's — to the grave. She was an odd old lady, but I liked her. I liked John, too, very much." She paused to make a neat row of stitches in the tulip quilt she and Emer were piecing for Hazel's second daughter, Pauline. Then she added, "Everyone liked our Little John, and especially the ladies."

"Aye." Emer laughed. "I did, and I miss him. He has a way

186

of lighting up the day."

"And we all know how you feel about red hair," Hazel said gently.

Emer pricked her finger and frowned as a drop of blood blotched the quilt. "Ah, glory be! Look at that."

"And you can't just conjure it away," Hazel said, half in question.

"No. It's too close to a living thing though no' . . ." *Sentient* was the word she wanted, but the subject was a complicated one. "Have you some soda water?" It wasn't what she used herself, but she knew humans did.

"Right here, my dear. That's not the first drop of blood to be shed in the stitching of a quilt, and I won't even speculate if fairy blood is any different in make-up to mine." Hazel leaned down and removed a siphon from her sewing basket. She added mischievously, "I don't need to speculate. Jim got his ghoulish hands on some of Matt's blood as soon as he decently could after we married. I think he had grand plans to see if your fairy immunity to disease could be passed on by transfusion."

"And can it?"

Hazel pursed her lips. "We think . . . I mean, Jim thinks, probably not. Matt can't catch a cold. The girls occasionally get a sniffle, but it goes away in hours rather than days. That suggests they have much better immune systems than I have. But, as to passing that on, except the way Matt passed his fairy blood on . . ."

"What is a transfusion?" Emer asked, belatedly.

"It means giving blood from a donor intravenously to someone who needs it, through accident, surgery or haemorrhage. It has to be the right blood type. The wrong blood can do a lot of harm. Fairy blood though . . . well, Matt's, if that is any indication . . . *has* no type. It should be able to be used for any patient."

Emer waited, dabbing at the blood spot on the quilt with a clean cloth.

Hazel went on, apparently picking her words. "Jim tried using Matt's donated blood, with Matt's full knowledge, obviously, for five patients in total. They all recovered well, but they still catch colds. The follow-up blood tests Jim did show them as one hundred per cent human." She shrugged. "It's a shame, in some ways, but, human nature being what it is, the alternative might be used to do unspeakable things.

"It seems the only way to get what Jim calls *the over there effect* is to be born to a fairy or part-fairy parent." She put away the siphon and said, "Not that Jim's the only interested medical man. There's a doctor in Sydney—Doctor Hanover. Jim found out he's been paralleling the research, using pixie blood.

"Now, what *were* we talking about before we got on to Doctor Jim Frankenstein-Dracula's experiments with my innocent fairy husband?"

"Little John, I think."

"Yes, and your penchant for red hair."

Emer took up her needle again. She took up Hazel's sly suggestion, too. "Hazel, you ken fine I love Rory and am faithful to him. I've never lain down with another laddie, and I never will."

"I never suggested you would. However, a lady, even one wedded heart, body and soul to one of the best men who ever wooed a woman, still has eyes to see, ears to hear and a heart to lift to a bit of borrowed sunshine."

"That's a grand way of putting it. John is borrowed sunshine. But there was never a word or a glance or a thought between us I'd hesitate to share with Rory . . . or with John's forever if he has one."

"If he did, he never told me about it," Hazel said with some regret. "He must be all of thirty by now . . . quite time he made some lady as ridiculously happy as you and I are. I'm sure he could."

Emer was sure he could, too. "He said, or implied, his father was still living, so maybe he went to him."

"Again, I have nothing to add, save what I said once before. John's father, or his real mother, may have been a child or grandchild of Elsie's . . . or a niece or nephew, I suppose. It really is none of my business. Oh, but why, oh why do we feel the need to pretend these things? John could not possibly be Elsie's son. She was over ninety if she was a day and ladies do *not* have children in their sixties."

Sylvan do . . . och, Elsie Folly could not have been sylvan.

Emer pulled herself up. "We don't pretend they do."

"No, *you* don't, my dear. It's humans who stir up all these mysteries." Hazel snipped off a thread with a pair of silver scissors and patted the quilt. "This is coming up well . . . and nice as Nancy's. Soon we can start on Carol's. She wants marigold colours . . . that's if you want to continue? I'd be happy to help you make one for Andorie, too, and for Davey, of course. Maybe something with beetles and cheese."

Emer smiled politely at what she knew was a joke. "I would like that. I used to make quilts with Mam. I miss her."

Hazel pushed back her chair and carefully gathered the part-done quilt into a cotton cover which she buttoned securely. "Let's have tea, and then I'll drive you back to the church so you can go home to your lovely family."

Emer nodded and smoothed an absent hand over her lavender gown.

"That's so pretty," Hazel said. She poured the tea and then said, over her shoulder, "Emer, are you expecting?"

Emer felt her lips tip up. "Aye. But only just. How did you know?"

"I didn't. I just wondered. You're *glowing* in the way expectant ladies are supposed to but rarely do. I remembered you said you'd like another baby and—"

"And I'm getting no younger. We decided the time had come, although it seems unlikely Flower will be along to keep her promise regarding the backaches."

"Oh dear, yes. Poor child." Hazel, who now knew the full tale of the expedition to recover Flower from *Fayhaven*, sighed. "I still feel rather bad about my part in that. If I'd put her in the front seat of the car, and stopped often, and had the windows down, she would have fared better. I virtually put her in the back and forgot about her. You and I got talking, as we always do."

Emer had thought of the same thing, multiple times, but she said, "She had only to ask you to stop. You did offer. Anyway, I'll still see my wee sister and benefit from her *loving touch*. Rory and I are going away to Erin a' Fee before the time comes. Rory said he can depend on Master Berryman and maybe your Matt to keep St Botolph's warm."

"Matt will be pleased to do it. I know he misses his time as a parish priest. He likes people better than he likes administration, although he's so good at it."

She handed Emer a cup.

After they had tea, she drove Emer to the church, as she'd suggested.

"I'll leave you here, my dear. Nancy and Beattie are at the pictures."

"Oh?"

"The cinema, I mean."

"Ah, Kerry took me to see a film when she sponsored me," Emer recalled.

"They're seeing a love story called *Violet in Paradise*. Matt and I went last week, and it's a lovely story with lots of dancing. I promised to be there when the movie finishes so we can all go for ice cream. The other girls are with Matt, visiting Gib and Avice — Matt's mum and dad. I like to make time for them to have separate treats. Oh dear, my Nancy is growing up.

Soon she won't want to eat ice cream with her old mum."

Emer reassured her friend that her Nancy would always love her. Then she got out of the motor car with the relief she always felt and walked over to the church. On a whim, she conjured open the door and stepped inside.

She was considerably surprised to see Rory kneeling in a back pew, with his bright head bent in prayer or contemplation. He often came to the church to spend quiet time there, but he sat in the choir seats, or in their family pew.

He's giving thanks for the new wee life we've made, talking it over with the Lord, just as I did with Hazel.

Her heart sang.

Not wanting to disturb Rory, Emer sank into her accustomed seat. He'd see her when he lifted his head, and they could walk home together. She gave herself over to the tranquillity of the place. She loved it for Rory's sake. She also loved it for her own. She thought the new bairn would be baptised in this church, but would Rory do the task, or would he invite Berry or Matt to officiate? Or, might they have the baptism at Rósanna Locha so Dornie, Lambert and Flower could attend?

One day, Rory would have a curate, but that was a long time in the future, and Emer thought she might not be there to see it.

"Wee Amber Pearl," she whispered. She knew she would have a daughter, with marmalade hair and different-coloured eyes, and if her first name was Amber, it followed that the other should be Pearl. One could hardly burden a wee lassie with a name such as *Mother-of-Pearl*.

She closed her eyes and weariness overcame her. She let herself drift. She'd rest in this lovely place until Rory was ready to walk her home.

191

CHAPTER THIRTY-ONE: THE PRICE OF A RING BOX

February 1959, *St Botolph's*

"Emer."

She lifted her head. "Aye?"

John Folly stood looking down at her with his sunlit smile.

"Greet you, John! I was talking about you today with Hazel."

"No wonder my ears prickled." He lifted one long hand and rubbed his ear as if it stung.

"Nothing bad was said," Emer assured him.

"I'm surprised. Some while ago, you gave me a commission, and I've taken a long time over it."

"Not to worry, laddie. I know fine you've had other things on your mind."

He laughed. "That's no excuse. *Laddie* indeed. I'm older than you, young Emer."

You are not.

"Braeside laddies are laddies from first breath to last," she said in excuse.

"I'm no braeside laddie . . . if I understand the term. That's one of the fay orders, right?"

"Aye. I'm almost pure brae, but for a spot of the green way in my blood. That's leprechaun, by the way."

"And Father Rory?"

"He's a wee bit brae, and a wee bit pixie and teg and

leppy . . . a wee bit other things — and a mutie on top of that."

He shook his head slowly. "I'll never get a grasp on all these things. Mum didn't know much — or didn't want to know. She wasn't pleased when I started to conjure, although she should have known it might happen. I was way past the usual age, as far as I understand it. If I'd never begun, I wonder if she'd ever have told me I wasn't fully human."

Emer said, "Some fay folk never do conjure. My father-by-love doesn't, being a green gossoon. And plenty of trace fay have no idea what they are. They just know they're a wee bit luckier, or healthier than their peers. But what brings you here, Little John? Hazel said you'd gone away."

His eyes crinkled at the nickname that had slipped out. "And you're Maid Marian? I don't see Father Rory in the role of Robin Hood, and he's certainly no Friar Tuck."

Emer shook her head at him.

John said, "I have gone away. I came back here to pay my respects to Mum's resting place, now her stone is set, and to pick up some paperwork she kept in storage at the bank in Appledore. Then I remembered your commission. It was well begun, but it needed finishing, so I put off the visit until I could bring the ring box to you."

"That's kind," Emer said.

John nodded back to the pew where he'd been kneeling when she mistook him for Rory. "I have it here. I was going to leave it by the altar because I knew Father Rory would hand it on to you. It's even better to give it to you in person."

Emer rose to her feet, and they walked to the back of the church, where John opened a large suitcase he'd left in the shadows of the pew. He handed Emer a brown-paper parcel tied with string and sealed with red wax.

She took it and held it, curiously unwilling to open the paper.

"Take it home with you and open it when you're ready,"

John said.

"Thank you. I'm sure it will be beautiful."

"I don't need praise or thanks. I have a talent with wood, and it was fun to make something different from my usual bits and bobs. It *is* beautiful, but that's as much down to you and Father Rory as it is to me."

Emer considered her next words with care. John had said he was around three-quarters human. He lived in the human realm and seemed to know little about his fay side. That suggested she should pay him for the box with human money. She had not brought any with her for her visit with Hazel, but she knew Rory had a box of notes and coins in the vestry.

"We didn't agree on a price," she said.

"You folk don't use money."

"Not at home. We do now and then *over here*."

"What do you do instead, at home?"

Emer struggled to think of that. The fay barter system wasn't really bartering as humans understood it. It was more a matter of gifts and vocation. She said, "See, if I need butter, one of the colleens from Crock o' Gold gives me what I need when I ask. I make salves and grow herbs and flowers. I give her what she needs when she asks."

"But you don't set the price ahead of time."

She shook her head. "There's no price. We give what folk want, or need. Sometimes we give something as a gift for happiness and that can be passed on. When I went to my wedding with Rory, I wore a gown a dear friend made for me. She said I could offer it to my daughters in their turn."

"Daughters?"

Emer sidestepped the implied question. "She was sure I'd have a lassie someday. But that's the way it works *over there*. I ken fine it works in other ways *over here*. The person with the goods or the skills fixes on a price, and the person who wants the goods or the work pays it."

"That's more or less right, although it doesn't take auctions and market haggling into account. How about I tell you what I would like to have, and you tell me if it is a fair price for a ring box?"

Emer waited, piecing this out in her mind. "Aye."

"Well then, maybe we could go out under the oak tree. What I have in mind might not be appropriate for a holy church. Do you know the lines in the good book about the *den of thieves*?"

"I do."

"I think Father Rory might have a quite vigorous response if he thought I was transacting my business within these hallowed walls."

He picked up his case and Emer, carrying her parcel, walked with him out to the oak tree where he'd had his stall at the fete.

He sat down on the grass and waited until she joined him. "So?"

He said, "I like you, Mistress Emer. Not many ladies would be so composed in the circumstances. You're comfortable to be with. Father Rory is one of the few men I have met who must truly deserve a love like you."

"What did you want?" she asked, unable to respond to such an odd compliment.

"I want to tell you a story. That's all. It's an old story, and I haven't told it to anyone living, but you see, I'm going to be married next month, and I want it off my chest."

"Congratulations," Emer said. She wondered if the price of the ring box would be Rory's services at the wedding. If so, it would be simple, since Rory needed no payment in any case. She added, "Do I know your love? Is she fay or human or somewhere in between?"

"I doubt if you know her, and I think you never will. We'll be married in her home parish, and I will do my best to be a good husband and God willing, a good father. I've seen Father Rory and Bishop Charming with their children, and they are a fine template for me. I never knew my own dad, you see."

"I'm sorry for that," Emer said. She thought of her father, growing old before she ever really knew him, and she was glad he was such a kindly presence in her mind.

John said, "I'm in the process of tying off my former life. Not that I'm ashamed of any of it, but I want a fresh start with my new love."

"That's a fair thought. My mam wed a leprechaun man from Erin a' Fee after dear old Da went to glory. She lives with him there, and that's better than staying at the brae where folk knew Da." She waited.

John said, "I want someone to know this tale. Mum knew, because I told her, but only one other person ever did. I'd feel easier if someone knew, just in case . . . well, in case someone should ask about me one day. Mind, I think that's unlikely, after all these years." He smiled faintly. "I might have told Missus Charming, but she's a busy woman."

And she lives over here . . .

"Besides, she might feel moved to *do* something about it. You won't, I think."

"You should talk to my husband. He is a wonderful listener, and he has so much love in his heart that he never judges anyone."

"I know Father Rory was very good to Mum, but I want to tell a woman." He spread his hands. "Mum was my great support for all these years. She always wanted me to be happy, but I think she'd have been uncomfortable if I'd married while she was still in the land of the living. My wife would have felt she had a right to know some things Mum preferred not to speak about."

Such as your true parentage, laddie.

At one time, Emer would have never thought twice about

true parentage, but Hazel's matter-of-fact comments about genes and heritage and blood had given her new perspectives. Had she wed one of the braw laddies who had helped make her cottage, she'd never have had to consider any of her descendants might have cat-selves. It seemed to her that a human wife had even more necessity to know what genes might shape her children.

Think of a human lady's fright if one day her child manifested as a wee kitten! But maybe John's wedding a fairy?

"Tell on then." Emer set the ring box parcel beside her and leaned against the oak's trunk. It was rough, but it supported a tangle of honeysuckle which eased her back.

Chapter Thirty-Two: Just the Two of Us

February 1959, *St Botolph's churchyard*

John said, "When I was younger, I was something of a wanderer. A come-and-go boy, Mum called it. It bothered Mum, because my father was a wanderer, too. He'd wandered into her life and then off again before I was born. Or so Mum said.

"I was one of those boys who's a long, thin streak of wire and fibre, and I got into mischief as boys do. Mum moved about a bit, so maybe she was a wanderer, too. Every five or six years we'd up sticks and live somewhere different for a while. I got some schooling here and there. Mum worked as a cook, and as a housekeeper and did some bush nursing. She was *the widow Folly*, with papers to prove it, so no one worried much about me and my lack of a father. Once I got to sixteen or so, I think she expected me to start courting, but I didn't. I had no interest in girls in that way. And in case you think I'm queer, I had no interest in boys that way, either.

"I looked very young, but she didn't much worry until people started referring to her as *John's gran*."

Emer made a small motion with her hands, and John smiled at her. "Elsie truly was my mother. She was over forty when I was born, so by the time she was sixty, I was coming up to twenty . . . and looked, maybe, fourteen. I looked fourteen for a considerable time. I picked up some work as a tar boy — that's a shearers' helper — and other things. It wasn't a

198

bad life."

Emer stared at him. "But I thought Hazel said —" She shook her head. "No, she just said your mother had lived in this country for a good many years. Go on."

"Reading between the lines, I think Mum wasn't too sorry that my father wandered off. She may have expected it. I suspect she — um — made a certain use of him."

"Och, I know what you mean," Emer said, enlightened. "Mistress Pendennis, a pisky lady I know, is wed to a good man and has been for many years, but before that, she gave another good man a son. It was a favour by arrangement."

John looked relieved. "Then you understand how these things happen. Mum was a good woman and strongminded. I think she wanted someone of her own, to care for, but she also wanted to be in charge of her own life. If she'd remarried, then she would have had to fall in with her new husband's wishes, the way she probably did with her first husband's decision to leave Scotland."

"She could have gone back."

"I suppose so, but she never did. I gather she found the sailing hard to bear. She probably wanted a daughter to love, but she got me."

"Son or daughter, we love them just the same," Emer said.

"And you're in a position to know, with young master red and his sister. What are their names?"

"Davey, after my dear old da, and Andorie, who is named for my mam and Rory's."

"And the next will be named for your father-in-law?"

Father-by-love, he means, and not Lambert, bless him. Maybe, if we knew who he was . . .

"We're having another daughter one day soon," she said. She hadn't intended to tell him, but confidences were easy under the influence of John Folly and his *borrowed sunshine*. She glanced at the sun, judging the time remaining before Rory would expect her home.

John must have noticed that, as well as the reference to a second daughter, but he made no comment.

He went on with his story.

"So, it was Mum and me for a long while. In the ordinary way, I'd have left her and set up my own household, but we got on well, and it was just the two of us. I eventually started seeing girls at dances. There weren't many men on account of the war. I didn't join up, since I was fourteen when it started and looked younger."

Emer nodded absently, but her mind darted to the date. She knew the war had begun in 1939, the year before Dornie left the brae with Lambert.

If Little John was fourteen then, he must have been born in 1925 or so, and that makes him thirty-four, which is older than Hazel thought and older than he looks.

She turned her attention on him again, but to her, he still looked not much older than Rory. In that case, Elsie couldn't possibly have been as old as Hazel implied. Maybe a life of restlessness and hard work had aged her prematurely.

Seventy-five or so . . . Och, this is not my business. I think too much about age, on account of the years between Rory and me and between Da and Mam.

"I tried to sign up towards the end of hostilities, but they wouldn't accept my papers. They thought I'd stolen someone else's." He sighed. "I salved my conscience by growing vegetables while Mum knitted for the war effort. After the war, we moved again, and then we arrived back here, full circle, where Mum's husband was buried. By then, Mum was getting along in years, so she settled in as housekeeper to a widower. I did handiwork for him. Nice old man. He had no family, and when he went, he left the house to Mum. She was tickled pink. It was the first time she'd had a place of her own, so she decided to stay here. She said it would be convenient, so she could be buried with her husband when the time came."

"This is interesting, but I cannot see why any of it should

trouble your sweetheart," Emer said.

"None of *that* would, save for my lack of a visible father. I have his name on my papers, but since he and Mum were never married, I don't use it. I've never been sure if it was even his right name . . . though *Jeremiah,* the first one, seems likely to be correct. Mum thought he was using what you might call a *name of convenience.* Anyway, since Mum's gone, one might expect my father to be gone as well.

"It's this next piece that might not be what a new wife would want to hear. It doesn't reflect too well on me."

CHAPTER THIRTY-THREE: JOHN FOLLY'S ROSE

February 1959, *St Botolph's churchyard*

"Never mind. We've *all* had moments that did not reflect well on us," Emer said.

"Even your husband?" John asked with a quizzical smile.

"Even my Rory, once, but he *considered prayerfully* and came to an acceptance. And no, I'll no' tell you how it came about. I'm here to receive your story, not the other way about."

And besides, that is Rory's tale to tell or to hold close.

She bit her lower lip as a sudden thought struck her. *He should tell Davey and Andorie, once they're old enough to see him as a person and not just their darling dad.*

John took a deep breath. "Thank you, Emer. I knew you'd be understanding. It happened this way. I'd gone to a dance at a woolshed a few miles outside town. There was a swing band, and a barrel outside for the men, and tea and lemonade inside for the ladies. I'd travelled on a wagon with some other men, so I didn't have a partner, but I picked up some dances with single girls and sisters and cousins of men I knew.

"There was one woman who looked different from the others. She had on a dress patterned with tiny roses, and she wore rosewater perfume. She was a lot older than the other girls. She had brown hair, and hazel eyes and the most beautiful smile I had ever seen.

"I made sure I got a look at her hand. She wasn't wearing

gloves, so I saw she didn't have a ring. As soon as I could, I asked her to dance.

"Will you do me the honour, Miss Rose? I asked her, by way of pretending we'd been introduced.

"She'd been playing a wartime song called *Roses of Picardy,* you see."

"What . . . was she part of the band?"

"No, she just played the squeezebox for one set, standing in for a man who wanted to dance with his girl. I think he'd spotted his sweetheart being friendly with another single man, so he wanted to remind her to be friendly with him as well. Anyway, my Miss Rose played that set, and then she handed the squeezebox back to him and came down to sit on one of the hay bales they had around the walls.

"Right away, I asked her to dance, as I said. She said that would be nice, but she was old enough to be my mother. I told her my true age, which I didn't bandy about, and she laughed, begged my pardon, and agreed that she couldn't possibly be my mother. She had thought I was just a boy, you see.

"I said I wished she'd dance with me, because she was the most beautiful girl I'd ever seen in my life. I wasn't lying. Oh, she wasn't a girl in the matter of age, but she had a quality of youthfulness about her.

"She asked if I meant that, and I said I did, so she said . . . well, I don't intend to give you our whole conversation. We danced every set after that, and I fell in love with her, and her wonderful perfume, and her laughing voice. She was so *different* from other girls I knew, who smelled of cheap scent, or perspiration. She said I smelled nice, too."

"You do," Emer said.

"Mum used to say I smelled as if I'd just stepped out of a carpentry shop. In a break between sets, I brought her lemonade, but I don't think she liked it much. At the end of the dance, I asked if I could see her home, and she said she was counting on it. I had to tell her I didn't have a car or even a horse and buggy with me, but she said it was *just a step along the way.*

"We walked along a lane and up alongside the creek to some pretty falls. I couldn't see them well in the moonlight, but I'd been there plenty of times before. It was a picnic place, then, called Stepaway Falls. It's not there anymore. There was a landslide that knocked out the rocks . . . happened during a big flood that same year. We walked along some stepping stones, around the falls, and I remember holding her hand. I was trying not to slip and disgrace myself. It really was just a short walk, but I'd have walked to the ends of the Earth with her. We came out into thick trees. She took me to a cottage, and I expected to say goodbye to her at the door. She invited me in, though. When I stepped inside, she asked me if I wanted tea or something else."

He looked down at his hands and said, "I told her I didn't want tea. And — this is the bit that reflects poorly on me. I told her what I did want, only in a roundabout way so she could take it any way she chose. I thought she'd say *get along with you, do,* in an indulgent voice. I was reasonably sure she wouldn't slap my face. What I didn't expect was for her to laugh and kiss me. She said I was her wish come true, and that she'd *love* to lie with me.

"It wasn't my first time with a woman, but it was the first time I'd felt loved. She was a darling. She made it all seem easy and natural. Afterwards, she turned up the lantern, and she just looked at me for a long time. I remember she *thanked* me as if I'd given her a gift. Then, she kissed me. She said I'd better go and she'd walk me over the stones. She said she hoped I hadn't missed my ride home."

"Had you?" Emer asked.

"Oh, yes. I badly wanted to go back to her, but I thought that might make her feel as if she had to put me up for the night. Instead, I slept in the woolshed on a pile of fleece.

Surprisingly comfortable. That got me some joshing the next day, I can tell you."

"What happened next?"

John turned out his hands. "Nothing. I never saw my lovely Miss Rose again. I wanted to, of course. I went to the woolshed dance the next week all spruced up. I felt wonderful. I felt I'd — well, Mum put it best. She said I looked as if I'd *grown into my skin*. Even my hair was brighter, she claimed. I was going to ask my rose if she'd come to the pictures with me, or to have tea in a cakeshop, or — well, to go anywhere with me. I wanted to be with her, any way she wished. I'd have done anything she wanted. I'd even carved her a gift, decorated with roses, naturally." He sighed.

"I might as well have saved my best shirt, because she wasn't at the dance. She wasn't at the next one, either. I asked about, but no one knew her. They remembered her at the dance as *that woman in the rose-print dress who stood in on the squeezebox*, but they didn't know who she was.

"The band owner, a chap called Reg Campion, said he didn't know her. He said his brother Ray had been whinging about wanting a chance to dance *with my girl for a change*, and she'd just turned up and offered to play. *Like magic*, he said. He said he'd have her in the band any time she chose, and he asked me to tell her so when I found her.

"I decided to go to her house, on the pretext of delivering Reg's message. She'd invited me there in the first place, after all. I thought if she was out, I could leave her the note, and the little gift. If she was in, I could give them to her in person. Then I could tell her I wanted to see her again. Even if she didn't want to go out with me, I thought she wouldn't be angry with me for asking." He clasped his hands and looked up at Emer. For once, there was no smile in his hazel eyes. "I was not expecting her to take me to bed again. Not right away. Oh, I'd have jumped in with her in a blink if she'd offered, but I wasn't going to ask or expect it. I just wanted to see her."

Emer thought of herself and Rory. She couldn't remember either of them ever *asking* the other, or *expecting* love. Lying together was just what they did naturally, and often. She smiled and said gently, "She wouldn't be angry. She must have wanted to be with you or else she wouldn't have invited you into her cottage."

"So I thought . . . I went back to the woolshed and took the path to Stepaway Falls. I had the note from Reg, and the little gift, and a bunch of roses . . . I remember it was difficult to find enough in Mum's garden because it was the end of the flowering season. Mum said I was *overegging the pudding, lad-die,* but she was sympathetic, I think. She thought I was seeing a local girl.

"So, there was I, with high hopes . . . but somehow, I must have missed the turn. The place looked different in daylight. I went the way she'd taken me, but I ended up on a path above the falls. There were plenty of trees, but they were scrubby, and there was no house in sight.

"I tried again, that day, and at other times, but I could never find her house.

"Finally, Mum asked me square what was wrong. I told her about my rose, and she told me I must have fallen in with *one of them.* She meant a fairy woman. Oddly, that hadn't occurred to me. I can conjure, as you know, but I usually don't. Mum drummed it into me not to draw attention to myself. I didn't know any other fay folk at that time. That is, I didn't *know* if I knew any. There may have been some around, but if so, they were — what do you call it?"

"*Passing,*" Emer said.

"Yes. I understand why they — your folk — do that. In a way, I've been doing it all my life, trying not to draw attention to Mum and me because she so disliked being referred to as *John's granny.* I tried one last time. By then, I'd lost Reg's note, but I left the trinkets I'd carved for her on the path near the creek."

"More than one?" Emer questioned.

"Yes. I'd made another. They were made for *her*. I could never have given them to anyone else, and I couldn't keep them. They would just remind me of what I'd lost." He pulled a wry face. "Of course, that *one last time* wasn't the last, but when I tried again, the trinkets were gone. Then the flood came soon afterwards, and the landslip blocked up the falls, so I lost the only way of finding my rose.

"I went wandering again for a few years, but then Mum started failing, and I came back to live with her again. I met Missus Charming when I did some woodwork for the church, and she asked if Mum would like to come along to some ladies' lunches. Mum met Mistress Grene and took to her. That was a surprise, since Mum liked to keep herself to herself.

"They used to have tea now and then. Mum was a bit taken aback when she found out what kind of company she was keeping—that Mistress Grene is a pixie miss—but she'd mellowed a bit, I think. And somehow, I got dragged in to serving tea at your husband's ordination."

He stopped talking and dropped his gaze again.

Emer ventured, "I'm sorry you lost your love that way. Are you asking me to find her? And was her name really Rose?"

"It might have been. She never said it wasn't, and it seemed likely. She certainly had an affinity with them."

"With nothing more than a first name to go on, it would be difficult. If she's a tree maid, that would be her only name."

Not that tree maids often come this side of the gateway. And they don't always live in houses.

Emer tried and failed, to picture one of the sweet-natured treefolk she knew behaving as John Folly's Miss Rose had. A tree maid might certainly take a lonely laddie to her bed if she felt he wanted it, but she'd be much more likely to lie down in a thicket, just as she was. And besides, tree maids were small, barely reaching Emer's breast. John Folly was taller than the average human . . . easily as tall as a braeman.

"Was she a wee lady?" she asked.

John shook his head. "She fitted under my chin. I know fairies aren't really thumbelinas . . . obviously. But I'm not asking you to find her for me, Emer. Not at all. It's a long time ago. Now, as I said, I have a sweetheart I'm going to marry. I haven't told her about my rose, because that would just bring out unanswered questions. Linneas is a lady — she must know I've been around the block a few times, but she told me straight she doesn't want to know about every girl I've ever kissed. In return, I'm content to let her past belong to her. She's much younger than I am, but then . . ." He shrugged.

"I'm no' in a position to frown at that," Emer said.

"I wasn't implying you were. Oh, I can see you're a little older than Father Rory, but you're younger than I am, and my Linneas is — " He shrugged again. "When we're together, the years don't matter. She knows her own mind, and I love her dearly. I assure you — I wouldn't marry her if I didn't."

"What *do* you want me to do, then?" Emer asked, perplexed.

"Nothing. Now that Mum's gone, I simply wanted someone else to know my little mystery. And one more thing. If you should ever meet a fairy lady named Rose, who wears rose perfume, and sounds as if she's singing as she speaks, and if she's as kind and wonderful as I recall her . . ." He trailed off as if he felt tangled in his mind.

Emer waited patiently.

"If you ever meet her, you might ask if she remembers dancing with a young man who *wasn't* young enough to be her son. Remind her of the evening when she played *Roses of Picardy* on a borrowed squeezebox at a woolshed dance."

"I'll do that," Emer said.

"Don't look for her, and don't put yourself out with

thinking about this. But, if you ever meet her by chance, tell her John Folly sends his love, that he's never forgotten, and that he wishes her well and hopes she found the trinkets." He smiled suddenly. "You might have to remind her of who I am. I don't believe she ever knew my last name, and *John*s are two a penny. Mention the red hair. She wouldn't forget that. She made some joke about it, but kindly, as if it was a good thing to have."

"It's a very good thing to have," Emer said.

"Of course you would know, that since your husband and your son are so endowed."

John got to his feet and offered his hand to Emer. She took it, bringing the parcel up with her in her other arm. He smiled down at her. "Thank you for hearing me out, Mistress Emer. I hope you find the ring box worth the price of listening to my long and tangled tale."

"I'm sure I will." She stretched up and kissed his cheek, catching the warm scent of timber. It could have been cologne, such as humans wore, but she knew it was a legacy of his fay ancestry.

"I'll be off now. I doubt if I'll ever be back in these parts, though never is a long time. Please tell Father Rory goodbye for me. He was kind to Mum, and it was a pleasure to know him. He's a lucky man to have you in his life."

"I know I'm a lucky man, but you are welcome to tell me that yourself," Rory said. He'd stepped around the corner of the church while they were speaking. He put his arm around Emer. "Did you enjoy your quilting with Hazel, my queen?"

"I did, and then I met Little . . . um, John, in the church, and he gave me the ring box I'd asked him to make."

"I'd almost forgotten about that," Rory said, glancing at the parcel. He added, to John, "I didn't know you were back, John."

"It's just for the day. I came to tie up some loose ends before

I head north again."

"John is being wed, but not here. It will be at his love's own parish," Emer explained.

Rory said, "I hope you'll be as happy with your bride as I am with mine." He raised his free hand and drew a cross in the air between them. "Go in peace and walk in joy, John Folly, all the days of your life."

"Thank you, Father Rory. I'll try, and I couldn't wish you a better fortune than that, either." John picked up his case and walked away, with the lowering sun catching in his red hair.

"Those days are going to be long ones, I think," Rory said, gazing after him.

"*I'm* the one with *the sight,* my laddie," Emer reminded him.

"I know, but—John's a quarterling, isn't he?"

"Yes, apparently. Hazel says so, and I think John believes that, too."

"Elsie was human but unusually long-lived. I think John's fay side is probably sylvan, so he'll live on for a good while longer than most. Not as long as Asht and his family, of course, but long enough . . ."

Emer felt a small stab of sorrow for John. "If his love is human, or even fay, he'll outlive her."

"That depends on just how old she is, and how old he is now," Rory pointed out.

"He's younger than I am. He thinks he's older, but I did the sums," she said ruefully.

"So, he was telling you about his wedding-to-be?"

"Not really. He was telling me of a lost love . . . he wanted someone to know his story before he starts his new life."

"And while the poor man was pouring his heart out . . . *you,* my practical braeside lassie, were doing sums?"

"He said he was fourteen when the war started, so it was an easy calculation. I just had to add twenty years."

They turned and walked out of the churchyard and passed hand-in-hand through the St Botolph's gate. The mare, Dorcas, awaited them there, harnessed in a small neat buggy.

"I thought you'd like to conserve your strength after quilting with Hazel," Rory said.

"Oh?"

"The twins are down at the falls with the Peckerdale children and Peter G. Oh, and Joe Bakewell . . . that quarterling lad who's some kind of cousin to the Grenes. They'll be splashing about for hours. Hula said she'd watch over them."

"I see," Emer said.

Hula was one of the water maids. She had a fondness for the twins, and for Peter G. Emer knew she would care for their welfare as if they were her own children.

She stepped into the buggy and Rory swung himself up to the driving seat.

As Dorcas drew them towards the cottage, Emer broke the seal, untied the string and unwrapped the paper to reveal the ring box. She gazed at its beautiful finish, at the pattern of heather and crosses and catsear flowers, and the hasp, polished and gleaming. She opened it with care and saw that John had lined it with heather-coloured felt, held in place with decorative beading.

Aside from being empty, it was exactly as *the sight* had shown her.

Chapter Thirty-four: Unicorn

June 1959, *Unicorn, en route to Erin a' Fee*

Emer and Rory expected their new baby would be born in September, possibly sharing a birthday with the twins.

In June, therefore, Emer left the pixie forest for her second visit to Erin a' Fee. This time, as she had promised Rory, the whole family was going, sailing on the fair winds galleon, *Unicorn*.

Emer and Rory gave their cottage, and the house at the brae, into the care of Peter Grene. At fifteen, he was a self-possessed pixie lad, and he said he would be pleased to tend to the gardens and to keep the places warm and aired in exchange for the produce.

Before they left, they went to say their farewells to the Grenes, the Charmings and Jago and Emblyn Pendennis. Beattie Hammett, staying again with Jago and Emblyn, said she would have been pleased to mind the cottages, but Rory explained they had already invited Peter G.

"We could do it together, Father Rory," Beattie said, staring at him with her intent gaze.

Emer wanted to ask her what Red was doing right now, but she refrained. Instead, she glanced at Rory and saw he was considering the idea.

To her surprise, though, Emblyn caught Emer's eye and gave a tiny shake of her head.

Why?

Rory, always sensitive to atmosphere, must have noticed

the small exchange, because he smiled at the pisky girl and thanked her. He added that Peter G would probably ask his friend Joe for help.

Beattie looked downcast, but she came to hug Emer. "Give Flower a kiss for me, and tell her I miss her," she said.

"Aye, we will." Emer made no promises that Flower would ever visit Treborrow. How could she, when her sister's last visit had ended in a return to Rósanna Locha on the kelpie, attended by Glory-Be? Besides, Flower was seventeen. Beattie might be fourteen and had years of growing up ahead.

Emer pulled herself up sharply.

Think less of the number of years between true friends, you foolish lassie.

"Goodbye, Father Rory. May I say goodbye to Red, too?" Beattie asked.

Rory obligingly gave Red a chance to commune with Beattie and Jago. The girl stroked him gravely, and Red chirruped and blinked in the calming way he had.

The red cat next sized up Emblyn, who lifted an admonishing finger.

She smiled, then, and picked up Red. "You take care, my fine red friend, and come home safe. Master Floppy will be looking out for you."

Having taken their leave of Rory's mentor, the family continued on their way down to the pisky coast to meet the ship.

"I wonder what that was about, with Beattie and Emblyn," Emer said, as Rory walked her down to the bay.

"I have no idea."

"I'm not pleased to disappoint the child," Emer said. She remembered a troubling thought she'd had before. "She sent a kiss for Flower. Do you think—"

Rory laughed. "I do not. In a couple of years, Beattie will be going to dances *over there* with Nancy Charming."

"Or ceilidhs in the green way."

"Both," Rory opined. "And so shall we, when we come home. Ah, look—the longboat's coming. We're just in time."

Emer felt some trepidation as they were rowed out into the bay on their way to *Unicorn*.

"You've sailed before," Rory reminded her.

"Aye, to Heather Isle, but that's years back. Flower had no trouble sailing that time, or when she came here first."

"She was a child then, and things change quickly with children. You were grown."

"You've not sailed before, dear laddie."

Rory agreed she was right about that, but he looked relaxed and carefree as he sat, easily balancing against the swell, with one arm around each of his children.

Emer thought, with a flash of envy, that Rory could have balanced on the longboat's gunwale and still had enough attention to admire the fluttering sails, coloured butter-yellow and reversed with white, of the ship that stood out in the bay. He had catlike balance and poise, even in man-form.

"Red will enjoy the trip," she said.

"He can be ship's cat, Da," Davey said with his wide smile. At almost six, Davey's features were emerging from the round-cheeked appearance of babyhood. He'd developed a straight nose like Rory's, and he had hazel eyes like Emer's, set under brows and a mop of hair every bit as red as his father's. He had a strong chin and capable hands with an odd little quirk on one finger.

Andorie, who adored him, called it *Davey's magic finger*. She was an enchanting child, and Emer, while admitting herself prejudiced, thought her the prettiest lassie she'd ever seen. Andorie had no *magic finger*, but she claimed her silver pisky bracelet, hung with charms representing things she loved, was magic enough for her. It jingled on several notes, and Andorie and Davey had worked out how to play tunes on her bracelet and his silver whistle.

The longboat pulled on steadily, and Emer watched the great ship drawing near. The galleonfee sailors, with their dark curly hair and hawk-like profiles, sang as they rowed, and Andorie joined in with her sweet voice.

"Andorie," Emer said, worried they might take offence.

The helmsman flashed her a smile, and said to Andorie, "Sing on, my lovely." He added, to the other oarsmen, "We have a *danz damar*, here, lads!"

Andorie glanced at Emer for permission, and she gave it with a gesture.

Danz damar, as Emer learned later, meant s*ea-dancer*, and it referred to a lands-person who had an affinity with the sea. She thought her children would have a whole new vocabulary by the time they reached Erin a' Fee.

Galleonfee, somewhat like leprechauns, had a powerful sense of family. The twins, after the first day or two of the voyage, took to climbing the rigging and greeting the figure-head as naturally as the swarthy children did who lived on the ship. The galleonfee taught them patiently, and the children gained strength and skill each day.

Emer found herself adjusting easily to the motion and Rory, of course, had no trouble at all. Red spent time walking along the railings and sunning himself on the deck while Emer sat in unaccustomed idleness, dreamily enjoying the peace before Amber would be born.

She'd told Rory of *the sight* showing her the name, although she hadn't mentioned the circumstances under which she'd heard him use it.

He professed it perfect. When not letting the red cat enjoy the deck, he sat cross-legged by Emer, reading psalms aloud in his beautiful voice, or sketching his surroundings.

He still had his eye for form and detail, and his sketches of galleonfee children delighted their parents.

"They'll never have seen a camera at all," Emer mused. She certainly had, and Hazel had even shown her how to use her Box Brownie.

Rory said, "They never will, since they don't leave their ships . . . though I believe they grant shore leave to any who *wed the ship*."

"What does that mean?"

"The master told me that very occasionally a traveller or a port-dweller falls in love with a galleonfee man or maid. They'll never deny love, and so they bring the lover aboard . . . but they're fair enough to know anyone who weds the ship won't have quite the same connection as anyone *born to sea*. They give a kind of betrothal period to make sure the lover will be *sea-fit*. They also make provision for the beloved to spend time on land when they wish."

"What about their galleonfee husband or wife?"

"They don't go that far, my queen. That's why anyone who falls in love with a galleonfee is cautioned to consider long and well before asking to *wed the ship*." He sketched one of the sailors, a woman dressed as the men were, but wearing a scarlet sash around her hips. A great white bird came next, flying over the mast, and then Andorie, with her face alight with pleasure and the wind blowing in her cloud of tawny hair.

"You could have been an artist," Emer said. Even after knowing him for close to fifteen years, there were still things that surprised her about her husband. In all their years together he'd been busy with his crystals, his studies, his calling and with working with her in garden and kitchen. This must be the first true holiday he'd had. Perhaps it was the first time he'd ever had the leisure to draw as much as he pleased. She said as much to him, and he looked up with a smile.

"Not quite. Back when I was small—smaller than the twins—Mum took me *over there* for a while. She said she'd meant to take me sooner but—"

"But?" Emer prompted. He seldom spoke of Annie Inker-soll anymore. She'd been gone for more than half his life.

"I don't remember the *but*. Something about a gateway." He shrugged. "When we did go through, we saw all sorts of things. I suppose that was a holiday."

"But that was the only time?"

"Yes. When you were away in Erin a' Fee, Berry sent me out to be sponsored in Patterdale. Clover promised to tend the garden at your cottage."

"You never told me that before."

He grinned. "I didn't stay long. The people were kind. They were related to Father Baskerton, who was the bishop before Matt Charming. They were good to me, and they understood about Red, but I couldn't stay away from the cottage."

"I never meant to tie you to it."

"You didn't. I did it to myself. I told you it brought me close to you to be there, and I meant it. I had to come home, although I kept on making visits to my sponsors for a while. Berry said it was all for the best . . . I'm not sure why."

Emer shook her head at him. "Mind, I didn't take to *passing* so well either, though Kerry was so good to me. I hope we'll fare better being away from home on this trip."

Rory conjured his drawing things away and held out his arms. "My darling queen, we're not away from home. As long as we're together, *we* are home."

Emer rolled up to her knees and cuddled against him. "I think I'd like to rest in the cabin a wee while."

"Is your back aching?"

"No, I'm no' so heavy yet, and besides, Amber is just one bairn." She patted her unborn child. "I have a wish to lie down with you, darling Rory. Where are the twins?"

"Learning to whistle the wind from a galleonfee lad—

young Leif Sorensen. He's the master's grandson, so he told me. He further informed me that makes him a responsible person with a great many obligations, which he was honoured to put aside for the education of the *danz damar* and her brother."

He got to his feet, gave her a mischievous smile, and sank to become the red cat.

"Red, what are you up to?" Emer asked, as the red tom sat back on his haunches and gazed up through slitted amber eyes. "Red . . . *Och, Red!*" The name came on a wail of laughter as the red cat gave a prodigious spring, landed on the figurehead, rebounded and leapt to swing in the rigging.

"Oh, Red!" Weeping with laughter, Emer made her way to the cabin reserved for their use. She conjured off her gown and lay down in her petticoat.

After a few minutes, the red cat phased through the cabin door. It swaggered up to the bed, crouched and unfolded into her laughing husband, as bare as the day he was born.

"Oh, my queen! Look at you there in your petticoat, all big eyes and beautiful big bosoms," he said lovingly. He lay down, rolled over and gathered her into his arms.

YOU MAY ALSO ENJOY THE FOLLOWING FROM EXTASY BOOKS INC:

Elysian Games
Lark Westerly

Atalanta left Mel's apartment and scooted up the remaining flights of steps to her eyrie. Mel was too damned kind. He'd arranged for her to take over the lease of his cousin's cozy apartment when Helen eloped with her boy-toy from Troy. He let her use his shower when hers went wrong. He fed her when she was too wiped out to cook.

He was a great cook. She'd eat at Chez Mel more often if only he wasn't so damned cute and distracting.

Cute. Since when did serious athletes need cute in their lives? And now he was talking marriage. Marriage? Uh-huh. Marriage was spelled M-for-mortgage, A-for-angst, R-for-responsibility, R-for-reasons, I-for-issues, A-for-anger, G-for-green-eyed-monsters and E-for-exclusivity. All of which she could do without.

If only he wasn't so damned cute, she'd spend much more time at Chez Mel . . .but hadn't she just thought that before? There was no doubt that sex addled the brain. Even quickies under the shower.

Atalanta reached the top of the last flight and let herself into her apartment. Then she began to pack.

She was away for a week.

That was how she missed the delivery van that arrived at the apartment block at nine on Tuesday morning.

Someone was making free with her nipples.

Atalanta switched on the lamp and blinked. She'd half unpacked before falling into bed, but she was darned sure she hadn't left a half-dressed man strewn over the foot of her mattress.

"Get off of me, Mel." She was half laughing, but angry too. She pried herself away. Her nipple popped out of his mouth and he pouted.

"Aw, come on, Atalanta. You can't say you haven't got time now!"

Atalanta dragged a pillow out from under her elbow and swatted him. Then she sneaked a glance at the clock. "What the hell are you doing here? How did you get in?

Mel waggled a key at her. "You gave me this so I could water your orchid — remember? I was watering your rosebud, too."

"Give it back."

Mel stuffed the key down the front of his shorts. "Go fish?"

Atalanta looked at him with narrowed eyes. If only he wasn't so damned — oops! Been there, thought that. Still holding his gaze with hers, she extended one hand and made a sudden grab for the key tag where it peeked above the rim of the shorts. She tugged it free. "Out." She pointed to the door.

"Don't you want your breakfast? It'll give you strength for our three-hour nookie marathon."

"Mel, it's three a.m.! I've been asleep for three hours."

"Good things come in threes." He jumped off the bed and fetched a tray from the kitchen. Atalanta's eyes bugged as she took in orange juice (freshly squeezed), and three dozen oysters decorated with lemon and black pepper with a red rose lying tastefully across the shells.

"What the fuck is that?"

"Breakfast," said Mel again. He smiled. "I'm treating you like a goddess. I want you horny as hell so I can worship Pussy."

Atalanta sighed and pushed the tray away. "I'm not hungry and I'm not horny and I'm sure'n'hell am not a goddess. Go home."

"Can't I please come and cuddle—"

"No. I have to be up early."

"But it's Sunday! And you just got back. You've been away for a week. How many men did you pull? Tell me. I can take it."

"None. I'm in training."

"So? What's new? You're nearly always in training!"

"The men I met were in training too. No serious athlete will consider sex before a race. It slows them down."

Mel sighed. "Glad I'm not an athlete, then." He looked down at his shorts and patted his crotch with one finger. "Guess that's it, then, Herc. We're out of luck. Again."

He headed for the door, drooping. Atalanta sighed.

"Mel—"

He was back in an instant.

Atalanta got out of bed. She never bothered with night-clothes in summer. "Come on, then, if you want."

Mel's eyes lit up and his mouth dropped open like a kid who's been told he's going to Disneyland. He dropped to his knees and embraced her, squeezing her butt cheeks and pressing his face to her groin. "Mmmm . . ." His tongue curled out and lapped her gently. Atalanta gasped and gripped his shoulders. Her knees went loose and she would have sagged if he hadn't been gripping her. His tongue was sure and gentle, and she spun out in less than a minute.

By the time she was focused again, Mel was wrenching at his shorts. His penis came bounding free like an animated pogo stick, and she reached for it and ran her finger and thumb from root to tip. For a moment she was tempted to trade caresses, but why encourage him to dream of marathon nookie? She turned and leaned her hands on the bed. That was the quickest way to get him off—and off her case as well.

"I've got a brand new VR game," said Mel when Herc was back in his shorts. "Come and play with it in the morning? I'll make you brunch, and play you my new MP3s."

"I'm training."

"Please, Atalanta. Surely you can spare me an hour or so."

"No," said Atalanta. "Go home."

"You'll play when you have a chance?" he suggested.

"Sure. When I can make the time."

"I'll look out for you in the morning anyway," said Mel. "We could have a cup of joe and read the Sunday papers."

"No," said Atalanta.

"Marry me, then."

"No."

"Why not?"

"Why the fuck should I?" Atalanta took a deep breath. "Where's the rule that says I have to be married?"

Mel smiled.

"Why are you smiling?"

Mel's smile grew wider, as if she'd given him a present instead of a bend-over quickie.

"I'll be waiting for you in the morning," he said, and left the apartment.

Atalanta switched out the light and went straight back to sleep.

That's how she missed Mel's voice softly saying; "Gotcha."

ABOUT THE AUTHOR

Lark Westerly loves creating worlds and series where characters step in and out of one another's stories. When she's not orchestrating the lives of these characters, Lark enjoys walking with her dogs, cultivating her websites, and cooking her own recipe creations. Under another name, Lark writes children's books and runs a small manuscript service.

For more about *A Fairy in the Bed, Pixie Grip* and *Red Cat* series, visit Lark's website at www.larksinger.weebly.com

www.ingramcontent.com/pod-product-compliance
Lightning Source LLC
Chambersburg PA
CBHW070625130626
46556CB00001B/477